Worth More Dead

Worth More Dead

A Novel

Anne Katheryn Hawley

Traverse City, Michigan

www.conundrumbooksandmusic.com

ISBN: 978-0-615-63541-5
Library of Congress Control Number: 2012938668

Printed in the United States of America

This is a work of fiction. Names, characters, places, and incidents either are the product of the author's imagination or are used fictitiously, and any resemblance to actual persons, living or dead, businesses, companies, events, or locales is entirely coincidental.

Cover and interior design by To The Point Solutions
www.tothepointsolutions.com

To my husband, Jim, for all of his support, encouragement, and enthusiasm as I read each developing chapter to him. He is my biggest fan, as I am his.

***Conundrum*:**

A riddle whose answer is a pun;
A question or problem having only a conjectural answer;
An intricate and difficult problem.

Worth More Dead

Six Months Earlier

"Oh shiiiiit ..."

He frantically struggled to regain footing on solid ground. This explicative was followed by a very unmanly scream,

"NO-O-O-OOAAAAHHHH ..."

His arms desperately flailed as his body hurtled through the empty, chilled air toward the sharp, icy rocks below.

These would be his final words.

With a *crack* of his skull and *thud* of his body, his life came to an abrupt and premature end.

These sickening sounds were barely audible over the thundering noise of the waterfalls, but she heard them ... loud and clear. They would haunt her for the rest of her life.

As he went over the edge, their eyes had locked. It was the first, and the last time they would actually recognize one another, clearly seeing each other's weaknesses, failures, and sins.

He had seemed to be temporarily suspended ...

But it was just a moment in time, and it quickly evaporated with the mist from the falls.

On hands and knees, she cautiously made her way to the edge of the landing, stunned and absolutely horrified.

It had happened *so fast*!

His limp body seemed to be stuck somehow within the various rocks below, but his limbs, twisted, broken and bloody, bobbed as if in some kind of funky dance with the churning water.

Seventeen Years Earlier

Ginny was an awkward adolescent. She was skinny as a toothpick, troubled by bouts of acne, and had an overbite that required braces.

She was a difficult teenager, and that was putting it mildly. Ginny hated her life, and wanted to make sure everyone around her knew it. It broke Janice's heart, because until Ginny turned thirteen, she'd been the life of the family. She was always making up little dance routines, or acting goofy, trying to make people laugh. But then, seemingly overnight, Ginny shut herself off and stayed in her locked bedroom (which she hated), only coming down for meals (which she hated), and reluctantly going to school (which she hated).

She began to experiment with makeup. Her dad would wrestle her into the bathroom and forcefully wipe her face clean with a cold, wet washcloth until it was chafed raw, while accusing her of looking like she belonged in the red-light district. Ginny would scream bloody murder throughout the ordeal. Janice lived in fear and embarrassment that the neighbors would hear, but she never confronted Chuck. He ruled the house with an iron fist. He had raised his hand against Janice as often as he had the girls. Funny thing about it was that Ginny was like one of those blow-up clowns. Knock her down and she'd bounce right back up for more. The next morning, she would attempt to walk out the door for school wearing the same heavy makeup. Some days, if Chuck was too tired for battle, she'd succeed. He never could find where she hid the stuff.

Ginny would often seem to actually *look* for ways to provoke her dad. She'd saunter in after dark, when she knew dinner was promptly served at 5:30. She'd use foul language well within earshot of Chuck ...

She was once caught shoplifting a necklace at the mall. Everyone thought it would be a duel to the death. The skinny wisp of a girl and her lumbering overweight father were like watching a mosquito buzz around a bull. It was painfully comical, in a way.

At fourteen, Ginny brought home a mongrel puppy she found abandoned by a gas station. Surprisingly, Chuck let her keep it. This brought about an amazing change in Ginny. It was like she reverted back to when she was twelve. The puppy—she called him Barney—became her life.

Ginny took her responsibility seriously. Barney went everywhere with her, except school, of course. He slept in her bed every night and would lie on the couch next to her when she watched TV. She fed him, bathed him, and cleaned up after him when he had an 'accident'. Miraculously, her tirades and provocations sort of ... fizzled away.

Ginny's two sisters had little time for and little interest in the life of their youngest sibling. Cassie, at seventeen, was a misfit and a troublemaker. She spent as much time away from home as possible, hanging out with her worthless friends at the arcade.

Amy, the oldest, was twenty. She was the pretty one. Little Miss Perfect. She was totally in love with Billy, whom she had met in college. They were married and lived in a two-bedroom apartment. Billy used the spare bedroom as a make-shift greenhouse, taping tinfoil over the windows and installing sunlamps he purchased from a local department store. Although Amy didn't partake, she was enamored with this bad-boy side of Billy. It never occurred to her that this activity was actually against the law, and that she could be arrested if his little secret was found out. This was how Billy funded his portion of the bills.

Despite his *La Cucaracha* habit, Billy was pretty smart. In fact, he believed himself to be so smart that he quit college shortly after they had said, "I do". He felt that he already knew more than any stodgy old professor could ever teach him. Amy was majoring in literature, and made the commute between their apartment and Burlington College three times a week.

Billy's decision to quit was a source of contention.

When they had shown up at the house one day, *married*, nobody was surprised. Amy and Billy had gone to a Justice of the Peace because they hadn't wanted a hullabaloo made of any kind. Chuck and Janice were secretly relieved. Spending money on a wedding and reception was not an option at that point.

So, Amy and Billy's marriage just quietly slipped into everyone's lives. There was some speculation that Amy was pregnant, but this was not the case. They had done it on a whim.

Ginny was particularly enthralled by the idea of this. She loved spending time at their apartment and thought Billy was the coolest guy ever. Life at their place was so laid-back. Ginny wished she could live with them. To her, Billy could do no wrong. When Amy and Billy began having little spats, Ginny would always side with Billy.

~

One Saturday when Ginny was fifteen, Janice decided to take her youngest daughter shopping for new school clothes. Ginny had mostly worn hand-me-downs from her sisters, but with Amy out on her own and Cassie buying her own clothes with money earned as a server at the Big Boy Burger Joint, Janice felt she could afford this, plus, she wanted to do something nice for Ginny. This was a huge deal for the poor girl. Mom had never taken her shopping for new clothes. When they got to the department store, Ginny was frantically bouncing from one clothing carousel to another. It was as if she couldn't believe her good luck and was rushing around before the spell broke. Of course, nothing Janice picked out was anything that Ginny liked, and everything Ginny picked out, Janice didn't like. The day turned out to be a disaster. But that was nothing compared to what they found when they returned home.

As they opened the front door, Ginny expectantly called to Barney, who normally would be waiting right by the door for her return. Ginny started up the stairs, calling, "Barney? Where are you? Here, boy!"

Janice followed her upstairs with two bags of well-negotiated clothing. They both stopped mid-flight as Chuck came clomping from the kitchen, cursing, "Damned mutt! Crapped all over the place while you were gone. And he had *worms*! Slimy white worms in every pile of stinky shit. It took me hours to clean it up!"

Ginny turned, horrified. "Where is he?!"

"He's gone! And good riddance! That God-damned animal was constantly underfoot."

"WHAT DO YOU MEAN, GONE?!" Hysteria filled Ginny's shrill shriek.

"I took him out to the country and set him loose. He'll be better off—"

"WHAT??!!!" Ginny pushed past her mother and ran at her father, her fists pummeling at all angles. "How could you do that?

Where is he? You go back and get him! RIGHT NOW!" Her face was purple and contorted.

Chuck didn't respond the way he normally would have. Instead, he laughed, albeit a nervous kind of laughter. He grabbed Ginny's arms, pinned them behind her back, and shoved her up the stairs. "We don't need a damned dog in this house. He's gone, and that's that!"

He turned to stalk back into the kitchen.

Janice was dumbfounded. "Chuck," she whispered, "where did you take him?"

"Shut the hell up, Janice! Where were *you* when that mutt was shitting all over the house? I forbid animals of any kind in my house ever again, and I don't want to hear another word about it! Do you understand?"

From upstairs came the racket of Ginny throwing everything that wasn't tied down. She was howling like a dog herself … and then … silence.

Fifteen minutes later, she came downstairs with a brown paper bag stuffed with clothing and a toothbrush.

"I'm going to live with Billy and Amy," she announced as she grabbed the two bags from the mall on her way out the door.

After a short walk and arriving at Billy and Amy's, she was inconsolable. Billy offered to take her out the next day to look for Barney. Amy agreed that was a good idea. Surely, they'd find him ... Barney might even find his own way back home!

The next day after breakfast, Billy and Ginny headed out to look for Barney. Amy had laundry to do, as well as write a research paper comparing and contrasting Hemingway and Steinbeck. Besides, he was really good with Ginny; if anyone could calm her down, it was Billy.

They zigzagged through the many country roads between Burlington and Montpelier. Ginny was heartbroken over Barney, but also thrilled to be with Billy for the day.

Billy had the windows rolled down and Eric Clapton was belting out *Layla* on the radio.

After a while, Billy turned to Ginny, lowered the volume of the music and looked at her as though seeing her for the first time. "Hey, Ginny ... have you ever smoked?"

"You mean, like, cigarettes? Sure, I've tried 'em..."

"No. I mean weed. Pot. Hash ... the good stuff."

"Oh ... ummm ... I don't think so ..."

"Whaddya mean, you don't think so? You either have, or you haven't—in which case you've been missing out on one of the greatest pleasures of life!"

Ginny giggled. "Well, I would've if I could've. I don't know anybody who has some."

"Yes you do."

"Who?"

"Guess."

"You?"

"Yeah, me. And today is your lucky day. I am going to introduce you to your new best friend."

"What if someone sees me? Won't I get in trouble?"

"Nobody will see. I'm taking you to the falls."

So Billy and Ginny headed north to Burkette Falls, where history begins.

Burkette Falls had the reputation of being a teen hangout, especially at night. It was a beautiful spot located at the end of a dead-end road. You could hear the falls the minute you stepped out of the car. It took about ten minutes to walk the well-worn footpath to the top of the rather steep, rocky hill. You had to walk carefully because the path was right alongside the edge of the falls and one false step could have you plummeting into the cascade of water that crashed onto the rock formations at the bottom. The sound of the powerful water was both soothing and unnerving.

At the top was a boulder which was perfect for sitting upon, once you'd reached it. It was surrounded by a soft bed of moss. Unfortunately, cigarette butts and empty beer cans usually littered the area, making it less of a refuge than it could have been, and should have been. Occasionally, some Good Samaritan would take it upon him or herself to clean up the mess, but eventually it would be littered again.

Billy didn't mind the debris. He liked coming up here to "get away from it all". He particularly liked the fact that from the top, you could actually see the footpath, as well as the end of the road. You would know if anyone was coming to encroach on your solitude. So this was where he decided to bring Ginny.

Ginny couldn't believe she had never been here before; it was practically in her backyard. She had heard about Burkette Falls in the context of ghost stories ... something about a jilted lover jumping off the edge to his death and then haunting other young lovers who dared to venture up here. She had thought it was farther away.

"Can I walk here from home?" she asked.

"No, Ginny. It takes almost twenty minutes to drive here. I can always bring you, if you want."

Ginny found herself gazing at the water rushing over the edge, then splashing down to a froth on the rocks below. It was mesmerizing.

She could sense Billy's scrutiny, and began to feel the heat rise to her cheeks. She continued to watch the water, as her periphery noticed Billy rummaging into his pockets, pulling out a neatly rolled joint and a lighter. She caught the quick flame out of the corner of her eye as he lit it, then the reddened embers as Billy slowly inhaled the sweetly scented smoke.

She glanced questioningly at him as he held his breath, and then slowly exhaled through his nostrils. This struck her as pretty funny, or maybe she was just nervous. She started to giggle.

He held the joint out to her and murmured, "Puff the magic dragon ..." which made her laugh even more.

Billy didn't laugh. He just stared at her with his big brown eyes, extending the joint like a precious gift.

Ginny stopped laughing, cleared her throat, and reached for the joint, holding it between her thumb and index finger as she had observed Billy doing. She put it to her lips and pulled some of the smoke into her mouth, then quickly released it into the cool breeze.

"No no no. Don't waste this stuff. Look, Ginny ... like this ..." Billy repeated his initial drag, savoring it like a fine wine. He held it out to her again.

"Suck it all the way into your lungs, and then hold it there for as long as you can."

Ginny breathed in and out a couple of times, then put the joint to her lips again and sucked the smoke down.

FIRE in her throat! She could feel it in her ears, for crying out loud!

She burst into a fit of uncontrollable coughing. Her eyes were watering to the point that tears streamed down her face. Billy calmly watched her until the fit subsided.

"It's always like that the first time."

"I think that's the *last* time, Billy. That wasn't fun at all."

"Oh, but Ginny, the fun hasn't even started yet. Don't you trust me?"

She hesitated; then looked up at him as he smiled his perfect, white-toothed smile.

"Amy wouldn't—" she stammered.

"Amy wouldn't *nothing*. This is *not* about Amy. This is about you and me. I don't share this with just anyone, Ginny. You and me have always had a special kind of thing—don't you know that?"

What does he mean by that?

Ginny was already feeling a pleasant buzzing kind of calm. She had never felt this way before. She smiled weakly up at his handsome face, while wiping the tears off her own.

"Is that why you said, 'Puff the magic dragon'? Because it's like a fire in your throat?"

"Honest, Ginny. It's just like that the first time … because you have a … virgin throat …" He looked at her with a look of *sexiness*, not that she'd ever seen that look before, but she recognized it nevertheless.

"Ginny … are you a virgin?"

She began to feel very confusing feelings. While being petrified about where this might be leading, she was practically humming with the anticipation of it.

"I'm … ummm … I've … uhhh …"

"Here, honey, try it one more time." He gingerly held the joint to her lips; Ginny turned her eyes to his as she pulled the dry heat deep into her virgin lungs.

"Now, hold it."

She held her breath; then tried to slowly exhale through her nose, but again burst into a fit of coughing.

Billy chuckled, stubbed out the joint, and then pulled her close and held her.

It felt like an eternity, nestled into the warmth of his strong arms. She rested her head on his shoulder and kept her hands clasped together in her lap. She didn't know what to do with her hands. As she started to relax, she was filled with a feeling of carelessness. She thought about Barney, the reason Billy and her were even out together. Instead of feeling the intense pain and sadness she had felt before, she was calm. Ginny could actually picture him bounding through endless forests, making friends with the squirrels and birds …

He'll be okay. He's free in the wild! Maybe it's a good thing?

Her mind quickly came back to the present, with Billy's body heat and wood-smoky scent filling her up.

"You didn't answer my question," he said from somewhere far away.

"What question?" Her words did not seem to be coming from her mouth at all. It felt like a scene she was watching instead of participating in. It was immensely amusing. She laughed.

Now Billy laughed too, and started to gently tickle her.

"You know ... are you a virgin?"

"No."

"*No?*" He tickled her again.

"Yes."

She couldn't believe they were talking about this—but it felt so ... natural. She turned her face up to look at Billy's reaction to her confession.

He smiled down at her. Then, in slow motion, he brought his warm lips to hers, at the same time putting his cool hands under her shirt.

She was completely lost. She had never been kissed like this before. It was amazing. His hands were all over her, expertly removing her clothing. She wanted him ... had never wanted anything more, though this sexual desire was entirely new to her.

When it was over, Ginny felt like she was in a state of shock. It had all happened in a strange, fuzzy kind of blur. When he had withdrawn from inside of her, his whole body had convulsed several times as a hot fluid emerged from his hardened penis. Then he had slowly rolled off from her to the side.

The moss beneath her bare bottom suddenly felt cold, as well as the wetness between her legs and on her thighs and belly as it cooled in the wind.

She clung to Billy, shivering.

"Ssshhhh ... sshhh ... it's all right, I'm here. I'll always be here for you." He slowly rubbed his hand along the small of her back. "You're a woman now, Ginny," he whispered.

He dropped her off back at home.

"You can get your stuff later, Ginny. You should be here in case Barney comes back."

He's right. Of course he's right. Besides, I do not want to have to face Amy.

How can I EVER face Amy again after this?

She turned to the door and reached for the handle.

"Ginny ... honey ... we have something special. I never expected that anything like this could happen. I need to know ... would you be my secret girlfriend?"

She nodded solemnly, fumbled for the door handle, and stumbled out of the car.

Ginny opened the front door of the house as quietly as she could.

Thank God, nobody heard the door.

She stealthily made her way up the stairs and locked herself in the bathroom. She just stood for a minute, breathing ... listening.

She could hear Mom in the laundry room, moving clothes from the washer to the dryer, then spinning the dial till it clicked into place and the dryer groaned to a slow start.

She quickly turned the tub faucet on as her mother's footsteps padded toward the bathroom door.

Knock-knock-knock.

"Ginny?"

"I'm taking a bath."

"Does this mean that you live here again?" Mom asked gently.

At first, she pretended not to hear, then Ginny wearily responded, "Yeah, Mom ... I still live here."

The hot water started to steam up the bathroom mirror, which Ginny was vacantly staring into.

"Ginny, I'm so sorry about Barney ... and your dad ... he just can't handle having any pets right now. He wasn't really thinking about how he was hurting you. Ginny ... he's really sorry, too."

"No, he's not! Just leave me alone!"

Ginny stood like a statue until her mother's weary footsteps faded down the old, crickety stairs.

She adjusted the water temperature coming out of the faucet, took off her clothes, and wiped the mirror until she could see a blurry reflection of her naked body. Her face turned red as a beet as she contemplated Billy's man-hands on her nubby so-called breasts.

Amy has BOOBS! What on earth was going through Billy's mind while he fondled my stupid little pot-lids?

"You're a woman now, Ginny," he had whispered in her ear.

She didn't feel like a woman. She felt like … an idiot.

Did Billy mean it? Does he really want me to be his secret girlfriend? Amy is so much prettier …

Ginny just didn't understand it.

Why would Billy want ME?

Although … he and Amy really did bicker quite a lot.

She gazed at the mirror as her reflection was swallowed up by the steam; then gratefully turned toward the tub, and lowered herself into it, where the evidence of her afternoon with Billy vanished into the painfully hot water.

When she finished her bath, she threw her underwear into the tub, then wrung it out before tossing it into the hamper with her other dirty clothes. She often rinsed out her panties if her period had leaked from her pads. Mom wouldn't be suspicious.

She grabbed her robe off the hook on the back of the door and made a beeline for her room. She changed into a t-shirt and sweatpants, and then lay down on her bed to try to calm herself down. It wasn't long before she was asleep. She dreamt she was falling down the stairs in slow motion.

"Ginny!"

Her mother's voice woke her up just before she would have hit the bottom of the staircase.

"Ginny! Dinner's ready!"

She rolled off the bed, glanced in the mirror over her dresser, then made her way downstairs into the dining room.

Her mouth went dry and her heart started to pound as her parents looked up at her when she entered.

They know! She panicked.

"Pass the salt," demanded her dad.

Her mother passed the salt as Ginny slid into her place at the table.

She reached for the plate of pork chops, waiting for the tirade that she just knew was coming her way,

But ... nobody ... said ... anything.

Wow! She had gotten away with it!

Billy put forth great effort to appear nonchalant as he entered the apartment. Amy was sitting cross-legged at the coffee table, books and papers strewn about. She barely noticed him.

"Well, hello to you too ... and you're welcome for dragging your little sister around looking for a long-gone dog."

She gave him a passing glance, and then distractedly replied, "Oh, sweetie, thanks. Did you find him?"

"Amy, I said 'long-gone.' Do you *think* we found him?"

"Oh, no. I guess not. That's too bad. Is Ginny okay? And really, thanks for doing that. You know she adores you."

"Yeah, I'm aware of her little crush. She's a good kid. She was pretty miserable the whole time ..."

He debated whether or not to 'fess up about the pot, as Amy remained riveted by her work.

"Ummm ... I decided to give her some pot."

Amy quickly looked up.

"What? Billy, no! She's just a kid!"

"I swear, Amy, I think she's done it before, which makes it a good thing that I did. Now she can just get it from me, and we'll know that what she's smoking is pure. If she gets it from God knows where else, who knows what might be in it? I mean, if she's gonna smoke it anyway, it might as well be my stuff ..."

Amy considered this. Billy had a point. Just because Amy herself didn't want to alter her mental state didn't mean that practically the rest of the world didn't. Besides, Ginny was fifteen. She figured that it was better to have some control over what Ginny did. Billy would look out for her.

"I wish she wouldn't do it at all ... but if she's going to anyway ... I guess you're right."

"Don't worry, honey. I'll watch out for your baby sister. Hell, she's like a baby sister to me too."

Amy smiled up at him.

"How about I go take a quick shower and then let's order Chinese?"

"Sounds good. I am getting hungry ..." as her attention refocused on her work.

Billy stood there for a moment, waiting for some kind of clue that Amy might know what had really happened.

She was totally engrossed in her paper.

He turned and headed down the hall to cleanse his body and purge his sins, hardly believing his good luck.

And now, if Ginny decided to spill the beans, Billy could blame it on her imagination running crazy during a high ...

Present Day

Amy loved this time of year …October! The air was cool and crisp, and had lost that thick humidity that made you feel like your lungs were sponges soaked in tepid water. Not to mention that it made for really bad hair days. Now she could BREATHE! The leaves changing color were so beautiful. This was the time of year that she felt more spiritual, and definitely more alive!

She was on her way to pick up Will from soccer practice. Bobby was in the back seat playing his handheld video game. Technology … good thing or bad? Maybe a bit of both. It seemed to her that the boys spent too much time in front of the TV playing video games, but at least it was better than just watching the TV.

The stuff that's on these days! Kids are exposed to so much.

She thought of the organic shampoo commercial with the girl acting as though she was having an orgasm while washing her hair, and the commercials for erectile dysfunction, not to mention Victoria's not-so-secret… *Jeez!*

At least she made sure the games the boys played were appropriate for all ages.

Plus, they are working on hand-eye coordination … Am I making excuses?

This was usually the only time she could steal for herself during the day. While they were glued to the TV, she could take a long bath, or read her current book with a nice glass of wine, or work on one of her craft projects. Amy was good at that stuff.

Billy didn't get home until seven, which is when they would have dinner. Amy really enjoyed cooking. The problem was that she also enjoyed eating. She knew she was a little overweight, but now that the weather wasn't so oppressive she would start speed-walking every morning, and maybe even lift some of Billy's dust-covered weights!

Her job at the bookstore was only from 9-3 on weekdays, which meant the boys didn't have to ride the bus to and from school. The pay wasn't great, but the hours were perfect.

She thought about her secret stash of cash. *Whoa!* She almost missed her turn into the schoolyard. Sometimes she really got lost in her thoughts. Amy knew it made her appear spacey but she just couldn't help it. She had a lot to think about.

Will opened the door and jumped into the back seat.

"Hey, Mom! What's for dinner?"

"Hi, sweetie! Fettuccini alfredo and salad."

"Awww … could me and Bobby just have macaroni and cheese?"

"Will, there's hardly any difference between the two."

"Yes there is! A *huge* difference!"

"Yeah, Mom," Bobby added, "you always put pepper in alfredo and it makes me afraido!" He giggled and sent Will into hysterical laughter.

What a clever kid, Amy thought. *He's always coming up with funny things to say.*

Although he was younger, his verbal skills were much sharper than Will's.

"You guys make me nuts sometimes! If you promise that you'll eat all of your salad, I'll make you macaroni and cheese instead." She could just divide the cooked noodles and put a hunk of Velveeta in theirs. She was really looking forward to alfredo.

"Yay! High-five me Bobby-boy!" Will and Bobby slapped their hands together in celebration of their victory.

Lord, if it were only that easy to make Billy happy …

~

Billy pulled into the driveway of their modest little rental home. Amy had put out the Halloween/Thanksgiving decorations, and a pot of mums sat on each stair of the porch. It looked so warm and inviting, especially under the porch light, so why did he feel so uninvited in his own home?

He opened the door to the mouth-watering aroma of melted butter and garlic. His stomach rumbled with animal-like anticipation. Billy loved good food. Thank God, Amy was a good cook. For some reason, though, he never complimented her on it. Maybe it was because he felt that she did it more for the kids and herself than for him. Whenever she asked, "How'd you like it?" the best he could muster was, "My plate's empty, isn't it?"

It was just so hard for him to be nice to her ...

It was 7:30. Shit. He was late. Had it been worth it? Sure. But he was really hungry now. The half a joint he had smoked between Ginny's place and home had only served to heighten this sense of starvation.

"Hi, honey," Amy greeted Billy in her standard way. "Hungry?"

"Hi, honey," old habits die hard, they even called each other "honey" when they fought.

"I'm starved."

Wow, she didn't even notice that I'm late!

But then,

"The boys and I have already eaten. Your plate is in the microwave. If you want a salad you can make it yourself. I'm exhausted. After I get the boys to bed I'm going to bed myself."

So she did notice.

This type of passive-aggressive behavior, like not waiting to eat with him, was happening more frequently all the time. But what could he say? He didn't want to bring attention to the fact that he was late. Besides, he didn't really care. He just wanted to gorge himself in front of the TV anyway. She preferred her books, always had her nose in one.

He forced a smile. "What did you make?"

"Fettuccini alfredo."

"All right … well, g'night."

"G'night."

She turned to go up the stairs. "And don't forget to say goodnight to the boys."

She doesn't have to tell me that! Of course I'll say goodnight to my boys. Does she think she loves them more? Just because she works a short day and has the luxury of spending more time with them?

He bit his lip. He didn't want to start a fight. There was a plate of fettuccini alfredo calling his name …

A few hours later, Billy woke up. The living room had grown cold and he had a crick in his neck where his head had slumped over to the side when he drifted off to sleep. He glanced at his dirty dishes on the coffee table, thick with congealed swirls of leftover alfredo sauce. Ignoring them, he turned off the TV with the remote, and slowly made his way upstairs. He changed into a t-shirt, throwing his dirty clothes on the floor, and climbed into bed. God, his feet were *freezing*. He could feel the warmth emanating from the slumbering Amy. He slowly edged his feet toward her, trying not to wake her.

As his feet made contact with her furnace-like legs, she quickly kicked at him from under the covers and mumbled, "Jesus, Billy. Your feet are like ICE!"

That coming from the ice-maiden herself, he thought.

He curled himself into a ball on his side of the bed.

Amy woke up just before the alarm clock went off. She always did. Sometimes she would turn it off and gently nudge Billy awake. Other mornings she would pull the clock over on the nightstand as close to Billy's snoring head as she could get it, turn up the volume, and let it blast him out of his sleep. This morning it was the latter.

Maybe it will give him a heart attack ... Jesus! What am I thinking?!

Sometimes she hated Billy, but he was still the father of her children. She couldn't help herself. Amy often found herself thinking of what she would do with his life insurance money if he died. First, she would buy a house for herself and the boys, a real bona fide home! She would pay off the car and the credit cards, then put the rest, if there was anything left, into an interest-bearing account of some kind, which hopefully would be enough to live on. Then she would open her Arts and Crafts shop ... her dream. She could spend her days making wreaths, dried-flower arrangements, dolls, candles, specialty frames, and Christmas ornaments. Any money she made would just be the icing on the cake.

Billy's life insurance and health insurance for the family were the best things about his job. It sure didn't pay much but the benefits were pretty inexpensive and were simply deducted from his paychecks.

He has no ambition, she thought angrily. *He actually enjoys being able to write denials to those poor people who are filing claims for whatever catastrophe they're suffering.*

Well, it would be a good thing that if she ever did have to file a claim on HIS life insurance, he wouldn't be around to find a reason to deny it! And if anyone could find a reason to deny a claim, it was Billy. It was just the mean-ness in him.

It wasn't always like this. The memories of when they were friends, and when their relationship was fun were just so vague to

Amy now. It was like another life or something. Billy could be very charming. She had witnessed that when they were in public. The charm was just never directed toward her anymore.

When the alarm went off, it was so loud it even made Amy jump—and she was expecting it.

"It can't be morning already ..." Billy's husky, sleepy voice crept out from under the pillow he was using to try to drown out the sound of the buzzing clock.

"Yeah, Billy, it's morning." Amy switched the alarm clock off. She debated for a moment before deciding to extend a smidgeon of friendship, and then asked, "Would you like to go for a quick walk around the block with me before breakfast?"

Today she was going to start that exercise routine. It wouldn't hurt him to do the same. Maybe they'd actually enjoy it together.

"Are you nuts? It's cold outside, and it's still dark. Besides, I need to get to work."

Billy could see the hurt look on Amy's face. *But what was that? A look of...relief?*

"Look, I'm sorry ... I'm really glad that you're going. It'll be good for you. I'll get the boys up for you and give them some cereal ..."

"Thanks a lot," she said as she walked down the hallway to the bathroom.

Her mood changed instantly when she stepped into the brisk autumn air. The sun was just coming up over the trees and she caught a whiff of wood smoke. How she wished that they had a fireplace! Autumn in New England is what Northerners lived for. The colorful leaves were brilliant, the sky such a clear blue, though this early morning it looked almost purple-pink with the sun just coming up. She breathed deeply and stretched a little before starting her walk around the block. She wasn't ready for jogging, but speed-walking was better for your joints anyway. She thought about how funny she must look from behind, her slightly large derriere swinging quickly in that waddling gait this type of walking forced you into.

She glanced into the warmly lit windows of the houses she passed, wondering if every family was dysfunctional in some way or another. She thought of the boys.

Are they growing up feeling secure? Loved? Well yes, definitely loved!

She did everything for those two. She would do anything. They were the light of her life. The thought of them witnessing the fights between her and Billy made her cringe, but were the more frequent cold silences even worse? She wasn't sure how much they could sense.

Would it be better for them if she and Billy split up?

This was her plan.

She had secretly been saving part of her paycheck since she took this job three years ago, and had almost $3,500 tucked into the pocket of an old winter coat she kept at the very back of the closet. It was so ugly, no one would ever get it out to wear, not even her. It was a good hiding place. She had been very tempted to spend the money on occasion, most often at Christmastime or when the boys had a birthday. But Billy never failed her. Something always happened to strengthen her resolve and make her realize that she just couldn't live with him much longer.

She considered herself to still be fairly attractive. She thanked God, and Clairol, for her thick blonde hair. It was one length and fell to just below her shoulders. She most often wore it in a ponytail; somehow this style made her look younger. She would get compliments on her blue eyes, from complete strangers sometimes. She had always felt that her eyes had a lonely, sad look, very pale blue, with dark lashes that swept downward, and half-moons of vague, dark circles underneath them. Make-up helped hide the circles, of course, but there wasn't always time for that. Maybe she thought they looked that way because they were so much like her dad's eyes, and he definitely always looked sad ... unless he was mad about something.

In fact, her two sisters, Ginny and Cassie, had inherited those eyes as well. In them, she could see the ghost of her dad. Her memory of him made her feel one of two things: melancholy ... or anger. He really had had quite the temper. She and her sisters, and even their mother, had often been targets of his unreasonable and unpredictable fury.

Mmmmmm-mmmmm ... she didn't want to think about THAT right now. This morning was too beautiful to ruin with all these thoughts.

She suddenly realized that she hadn't spoken to Ginny in over a month. Ginny almost never called her. It was always Amy doing the reaching out. In fact, when she did call Ginny, the conversations were so exhausting. Ginny was so self-centered that unless the conversation was all about her, she lost interest. She would always manage to turn it back around so that it was about her again! She could drive Amy crazy, but Amy felt sorry for her. Here she was, thirty-two years old and had never had a serious boyfriend. And she acted like she was so damned DESPERATE! She might as well have had the word stamped across her forehead. Ginny had been in some nowhere relationships—a couple of married men ... and more than a few losers—the love 'em and leave 'em, one night stand types. She was cute, but really, *really* skinny. Always dieting.

Ginny was also always changing the color of her hair. *Drastically.* This had stripped it of its health. Amy had warned Ginny of this, telling her time and time again,

"Leave it blonde and just touch up the roots!"

But did she listen?

No.

Ginny also used very heavy makeup. Again, Amy had tried to give her sisterly advice (in a loving way) to tone it down. After all, did she WANT to look like a tramp?

Amy's thoughts turned to the other black sheep of the family. If Cassie hadn't had Dad's eyes, Amy would have wondered if she was even related. Cassie was thirty-six, but for all intensive purposes she was more like a thirteen year-old, hormones and all. She had done some serious drugs while in college (which she never finished, not that it would've done much good), that had obviously done some damage. She was not right.

She, too, had only nowhere relationships. The last one was actually a homeless drifter! That was when Mom had stepped in and made Cassie move back home, which is what Cassie had wanted all along. Amy wondered if there was some psychosis along with the drug-induced brain damage. Cassie was unpredictable and would sometimes just babble about totally unrelated subjects. She would fly off the handle for no apparent reason, very reminiscent of Dad.

Mom had her hands full, but didn't seem to mind. She needed to be needed; Cassie fit the bill.

Since living with Mom, Cassie had become quite plump. She insisted on keeping her hair cut so short that it almost looked like a crew-cut, and what was left of it she dyed jet-black. Her complexion was pale, which she enhanced by an almost white face powder. With her haunting eyes, Cassie looked as scary as she behaved.

Amy felt a stab of guilt at the shame she felt regarding her little sister. Both of them, Ginny and Cassie, were so screwed up.

Poor Mom!

Amy would go see her this weekend.

At least she'll see that she has one normal daughter!

The weekend arrived quickly. As it happened, Saturday was Halloween. Amy decided to take Will and Bobby to her mother's because she lived in a much better neighborhood. She could take the boys trick-or-treating there and not have to worry so much about checking the candy they got. They'd spend the night, and return home Sunday afternoon after dinner.

Amy was packing overnight bags on Saturday morning, when Billy thumped his way back upstairs after his Saturday morning ritual of reading the paper while drinking two pots of coffee.

"What are you doing?" he demanded. For a brief moment he felt panic. Was she leaving him? Had she found something out?

"Damn it, Billy. Don't you ever listen to a word I say? I told you two days ago that I was going to Mom's to let the boys trick-or-treat there."

As an afterthought, she added, "You could come too, and take them around the neighborhood while I spend time with Mom ..."

"Oh ... yeah ... well, Jesum Crow, I forgot ... that was *two days ago* that you mumbled something about that. I get the feeling that you'd rather I *not* go with you; so I don't think I will."

"Billy, you're just saying that so you won't have to feel guilty about me having to take the boys trick-or-treating by myself."

The thought of keeping those two, especially wild-child Bobby, corralled in the dark with all those millions of ghosts, goblins, Freddy Kruegers and whatever, hadn't actually occurred to him. But she was right.

"Can't Cassie go with you?" he asked, and then, "Hey, she won't even have to dress up ..." He looked at her with a smug, stupid grin.

As if she was supposed to laugh at that.

"You can be a real ass sometimes. You'd better not say anything like that to the boys. They'll think it's funny and just might try to tease her about it. How do you think that would make her feel?"

"Yeah ... whatever. Is Ginny going too?"

"I dunno. I doubt it. I actually hope not. I certainly don't feel like being a referee this weekend. I have to do that enough right here at home. It would be nice to spend a little time with Mom without a lot of controversy. Having Cassie there is bad enough."

"Yeah! See why I don't want to go?"

"Billy, you never want to do *anything*."

They stared each other down for a moment or two, and then,

"I want to do something right now ..." He gave her that 'sexy (but only in Billy's mind) look'. "The boys are raking leaves out back ..."

The suggestion, always out of left field, only annoyed her. Their relationship was *not* good. They rarely got along. Did Billy think sex was her wifely duty or something?

But she really didn't want to piss him off either. Maybe if she did give him what he wanted he'd get some much-needed work done around the house this weekend. She guessed it wouldn't hurt to give in every once in a blue moon ...

"Okay, Billy, but we've got to hurry. The boys could come back inside any minute, and I've got to finish packing."

Billy was already throwing his sweats and underwear on the floor, and climbing into the still unmade bed. As he did so, he knocked the open suitcase off; its contents dumped to the floor.

"Damn it, Billy! What's wrong with you? Did you not SEE the suitcase on the bed? What? Are you BLIND?"

There! That's that.

She was out from under the obligation and it was his fault. She stormed out of the room.

Billy lay there for a minute, staring at the ceiling. Bitch! He really didn't want her anyway. She just happened to be there.

Why couldn't she have had the frigging suitcase on the chair instead of the damned bed? Fine! Just fine!

His erection slowly collapsed to a state of defeat. His heart was beating fast in his chest, and he felt an ache—a hollow, lonely feeling—deep within it. His throat tightened and his eyes watered. "She fuckin' hates me," he whispered to the walls. He felt sorry for himself ... and then, "Well, I fuckin' hate her too!"

The drive to her mother's was only about twenty minutes, but long enough for Amy to calm herself down.

Why does Billy try to push our sexual relationship like that? It really doesn't happen all that often, but when it does, it's always so out of place, so poorly timed. But was there ever a good time?

No.

Amy desperately wished things were better between them. She felt that Billy was attractive, but she just wasn't attracted to him, not even slightly. In fact, he repulsed her. He had let her down on so many levels. Their financial life had always been a struggle. During the years when they had tried to have a child, sex had only served as a disappointment. It had become a stressful act. It had just gotten worse over the years.

Will had been such a surprise. Unfortunately, he hadn't been 'made from love', but he had certainly filled her life back up with love since he was born. Both he and Bobby. If it hadn't been for the boys, she would have left Billy long ago. She wondered if those miraculous pregnancies were some kind of sign that she was supposed to stay. But if that were true, then why was their marriage so lousy? She had prayed about it over the years, begging God to help her make it a better relationship. She tried, she really did. She knew she was a great mom, a good cook, kept a nice home, and she worked and brought money in to help pay the bills, which she kept track of and paid every month. She practically took care of the boys by herself.

What the hell does Billy do? Works his dead-end job making other people miserable, comes home, eats, sleeps, farts, burps, and then goes to that dead-end job again.

No wonder their marriage stunk!

The scales of responsibility are definitely unfairly balanced. I carry the load!

Her rebuff of Billy this morning was justified.

How could he expect anything else?

Seeing Mom was always a mixed blessing. It irked Amy to no end to see Cassie lounging around while Mom took care of everything. She cooked, cleaned, did Cassie's laundry ... and didn't even make Cassie pay rent!

Cassie was one of those dead-weight adult children, shamelessly living off their parents, with no future—and not even caring.

It was unhealthy ... for both of them. In a sick way they served each other's needs.

Cassie scared Amy. Her sister could transform from a child-like lamb into the she-devil herself in the blink of an eye! She blamed Mom for anything and everything, from how fat she was, to not being able to find her peace-sign t-shirt when she wanted to wear it. Cassie's angry tirades were a sight to see. Amy actually worried about coming to visit Mom one weekend and finding her bludgeoned to death by a spatula or something.

Really! You had to see it to believe it!

Whenever Amy shared her concerns about Cassie, she'd get shut down immediately.

"Oh, Amy, you don't know what it's like for poor Cassie. I mean, look at you. You're beautiful, and married with a family and a life ... can't you stop being so judgmental? Just where do you expect Cassie to go? She needs me ..."

Then she'd tear up and her chin would quiver.

For crying out loud, Amy would think. Honestly, it did no good for her to say anything. And God forbid if Cassie would catch a word of a conversation like this. The shit would hit the fan, and Amy would fear for her own safety. It was better all around if they just talked about the weather or something during her visits. Family get-togethers were always so volatile, especially if both Cassie and Ginny were there.

Thank God that Ginny wasn't coming this weekend.

Mom had a way of making Amy feel like a little kid again due to the fact that she wouldn't let Amy lift a finger when she was there. Mom would gently *shoosh* her out of the kitchen, and the next thing Amy knew, Mom would call out, "Dinner's ready!" Everyone would file into the dining room to a set table piled with food. Mom loved to cook, but wouldn't share her kitchen. It was a wonder that Amy ever learned how to do anything domestic at all. Either Mom thought she could just do it better herself, or didn't want to take the time to teach her then-teenager daughters how to do anything. Maybe it was, and still is, a control issue.

Whatever it was, it made Amy feel one of two things when she was at Mom's: either blissfully spoiled, or shamefully incompetent. But she never had a choice. Mom's house was Mom's house! Amy couldn't understand how Cassie could live with herself under Mom's roof like that.

And so it starts …

"Who died and made YOU queen?"

Oh great, Cassie's in one of her moods again. This is going to be a lovely weekend.

Amy and the boys had just been shooshed out of the kitchen and into the living room. Cassie had actually been flipping through a magazine when Amy had entered the living room with the boys. Her asking the question, "What else is on?" referring to the blaring TV seemed like an innocent enough question, especially considering that it was to benefit the kids, not Amy.

"Cassie, you're not even watching this …"

"How do you know I'm not watching it? You just walked in!"

Amy was not going to be sucked into a fight so shortly after crossing the threshold.

"Boys, why don't you go outside and get some leaves together to make a scarecrow?"

This was a roundabout way that Amy could get the boys to willingly, although unwittingly, help rake leaves. Besides, it was a beautiful day. They didn't have to be asked twice, but then—

"Hey, guys. I have some scary Halloween movies we can watch. Let's make some popcorn …" spoken sweetly from Cassie's lips.

Not wanting to push Cassie even an inch, Amy bit her tongue. Instead of responding the way she wanted to, she pasted a smile on her face and said brightly, "Ooooh … that's a great idea." It didn't matter that it was 11:30 in the morning and way too nice outside to be inside.

Sometimes being around Cassie reminded Amy of the *Twilight Zone* episode about the kid who had the power to annihilate anyone who questioned him, and all the people around him, including his parents, walked on eggshells, telling him that anything he said or did was, "Good! Real good, Anthony!" You never would have thought that anyone could be that way in real life, but Cassie was.

Dad had been that way too.

"I don't think I can live like this anymore. Damn him!" Ginny anxiously tossed in her bed, the sheets bunching around her legs, binding her in sleep-deprived loneliness. She thought of Amy, her sweet, stupid, blind sister.

After all this time, how could she not know what her own husband is up to?

Ginny's attention was drawn to her computer screen. Neon letters in the right-hand corner blinked: "You have one new message."

She disentangled herself from the sheets and stumbled to the desk. Her sleeping pills, coupled with her anti-anxiety meds, definitely made her tired, as well as slightly unsteady on her feet. But her mind, and quite possibly her guilt, kept her awake night after night.

This incoming message let her know that Billy must be suffering the same fate.

Good God! He took more numbing drugs than anyone she knew of, but they didn't seem to faze him either. Although her shrink prescribed her plenty, Billy often "rewarded" Ginny with other good stuff.

With a punch to the mouse, his message flashed on the screen. "I'm thinking about you. I'm going to get in trouble at work because I can't stop looking at the picture you sent me."

He loved the nude pictures she emailed him ... and Ginny loved sending them, in a naughty, thrilling kind of way. What the hell was wrong with her?

"Amy's sleeping. And snoring. The kids are asleep too, of course. I need you bad right now. I'm gonna pull up my favorite picture and pretend that you're here."

She knew which picture he meant. The one where she was on her knees, turning back to look at the camera from behind. She also knew what he was going to do while he looked at it. Leered at it, more likely ... *The lecher.* Still, it excited her. Ginny was more addicted to Billy than the drugs.

He signed off with: "We need to run away together."

That was it. He never signed his name. It was as though he was in denial that it was himself or something.

Impulsively she typed: "Enjoy yourself. I'm thinking about you too." She wanted so badly to add: "I love you" but those words had never been spoken between them. She left it at that. She was elated! He was thinking about her … actually getting off on her image!

Is he actually in the same room as the sleeping Amy? He is so bold.

She climbed back into bed and dozed fitfully for the remaining three hours before the alarm clock screamed out the arrival of morning.

Time to get up for work. This was always when she was the most tired; when she felt she could finally get some real sleep. Ginny worked rotating shifts at Mercy Hospital, and it was funny, but the only mornings she felt this way were the mornings when she was working the day shift. Figures.

Nonetheless, today held some inspiration for her. She actually had something to look forward to at work: an older, but handsome, doctor had been flirting with her. Sure, he was engaged to someone else, living with her in fact, but Ginny was starting to think that she had a chance. That would serve Billy right. She would marry a doctor. She was going to look good today! She had purchased some new shirts the other day, just for him. The necklines scooped low and the material was clingy—borderline pass-hospital-dress code. She would wear a lab jacket, but only when her nurse manager was around. The rest of the time she would leave the jacket off, and then say that she was "hot" if anyone had the nerve to say something to her. Yeah, she was hot all right! Hot for Dr. Gilmore!

She worked with a bunch of bitches. It seemed like everywhere Ginny had worked she was stuck with bitches. Probably just jealous of her.

Getting ready, for anything really, was always difficult for Ginny.

Why they make these huge mirrors, like the one in this bathroom, and those in all the department stores, I will never understand. They distort your image!

She absolutely hated the way she looked in them. If she even so much as caught a glimpse of herself in one, it would ruin her day.

After taking a shower, the big mirror was always steamed up anyway. She would put on her makeup using a hand mirror that she could hold at just the right angles.

Am I really good-looking … or just plain ugly? Ginny went back and forth on that one, and sometimes she just didn't know. Well, if Billy loved her, and even though he never said it, he *must* … then she had to be attractive.

Their affair, if you could call it that, had been going on for seventeen years now, off and on. It was hard to imagine that she was a mere fifteen when things had started between them. He and Amy had only been married for about two years. Now, she was thirty-two. Of course, Billy had to be in love with her. How else could he keep this going for so long? How many times had he said they would run away together? True, the sex was a little bit on the sleazy side, but beautiful-sleazy. He loved it when she performed oral sex on him; in fact, that was how it usually went. She hated how, afterwards, he would always be in such a damned hurry to leave.

Slam, bam, thank you, ma'am.

He would leave her with a little bag of pot.

Gee … thanks.

She did enjoy a joint in the following solitude. It helped diffuse the pain.

But now, yes … now Billy had a rival! Ginny could sense it. Dr. Gilmore really liked her, and definitely found her attractive.

Why else would he flirt so?

In the cold corridors of the hospital, her shift dragged. It seemed like every time she looked at the clock, only five minutes had passed. Sure, Ginny was busy enough, but she hadn't seen Dr. Gilmore at all today.

Maybe his patients are on another floor?

After all, she'd had the past two days off. Maybe he didn't see any reason to admit his patients to her floor if she wasn't working.

Or maybe that phony-sweet battleaxe down in Admitting has something to do with it.

Ginny was sure that if Dr. Gilmore had his way, all of his patients would be on her floor.

What John Gilmore lacked in looks, he carried in abundance in charm. He wasn't homely by any means—but his fifty-four years had taken their toll: a stubborn potbelly and thinning gray hair. But the 'MD' following his name made these minor flaws invisible. All of the nurses loved Dr. Gilmore and boy, did he love them back, professionally speaking, of course. In fact, the more they loved him, the better they took care of his patients.

Anyway, it was all in fun. He was a big flirt and good at it. Brenda understood and accepted this. John didn't know of any other woman who could handle marrying someone like him. God, he adored her! Vivian, his first wife, had not been able to handle the flirting. Their divorce was fairly amicable, no children, and he had been more than generous in the settlement. Now he was starting a new life. What was that Billy Joel song?

"... New life, new wife, and the family is fiiine ..."

Establishing a satellite office only thirty miles outside of Burlington had opened many doors for him. A whole little town needing his expertise with their aches and pains. The new hospital, although small, had a competent staff. He could admit his patients there when necessary. These small-town folks didn't like the idea of a big-city hospital. He actually enjoyed the time he spent at Mercy. He might decide to spend three days a week at Mercy and two days in Burlington if things picked up.

He smiled as he entered the admitting area. There sat little, old Gladys, always pleasant, an excellent admissions receptionist for the facility.

"Gladys! The love of my life that got away! How are you today, sweetheart?"

She giggled like a schoolgirl, flushed to a vivid pink, and in her sing-song warbly voice replied, "Oooohh, Dr. Gilmore, you are toooo kind! I'm well, yes, very well, thank you! And how are youuuu?"

He had only two patients at Mercy today. One was on the Renal Unit for a shunt placement and to start dialysis; the other was on the medical floor recuperating from pneumonia. Being in general practice gave John the opportunity to be involved with a myriad of ailments, and to benefit from the expertise of the specialists to whom he referred his patients when necessary.

He'd visit the pneumonia patient last. She was a talker! Being here in the hospital was her social event of the year, he thought sadly ...

The Renal Unit was small. The two nurses on duty looked up from their desks as he walked into the nurses' station. He smiled, waved hello, and proceeded to his patient's room. Shelley, a very serious middle-aged nurse with a slight limp, called to him as he reached the door. "Dr. Gilmore, I was just going to call you. I know that Mr. Gregory's dialysis is set for tomorrow, but his blood pressure has been climbing all day. His lab work from this afternoon looks like we may have to get him in for dialysis tonight."

He studied the page she had thrust in front of him.

"Shelley, thank you. I believe you're right. Bring me the chart and I'll write the orders while I'm in the room. Brains as well as beauty! I'm impressed!"

Shelley beamed. "I'll get the chart right away!"

He watched her walk back down the hallway with a bit of a skip in what was usually a laborious effort.

"He is one of the nicest doctors!" Shelley said to Cathy, her coworker. "And he's really good with the patients too."

Cathy smiled wryly and nodded. "Yeah, I like him, but he sure puts it on thick sometimes ..."

A short time later, he made his way to the medical-surgical floor. He glanced at his watch. Day shift was over. The evening crew would be here. He couldn't help feeling slightly relieved. That one nurse—Ginny was her name, made him uneasy. She looked at him with such intensity; yet acted so nervous around him. He'd have to try a little harder to break the ice with her. Hopefully it wouldn't take too long. This was the floor where he would most often be admitting his patients. He wanted to feel totally comfortable here. If anyone could make a young woman feel at ease, it was John Gilmore!

Billy pretty much liked his job dealing with insurance claims. They were forwarded to him after their initial denial. He was the second in line for resubmitted claims which he researched to find even a shred of further deniability, which he would concisely put into letter form and send right back to the still-hopeful policy holder.

Ha-ha!

He was good at it, but couldn't stand being in this damned rat-hole of an office all day. There were no windows, just the barely perceptible buzz of the fluorescent lights above. However, he was able to access the Internet; so he could enjoy his porn without interruption. It was a delicate balance, getting his work done while breaking the monotony with his favorite hobby.

Are there actually female specimens that look like these babes I can pull up on the screen?

He had heard that the images were touched up, airbrushed, or whatever ...

But man! In real life, good-looking women seem few and far between. They're either fat or just butt-ugly, not to mention that most are bitches from the depths of hell.

He thought of Amy, the drill sergeant.

She has sure put on some pounds since we were married.

He had been telling her for years that she needed to lose weight, but it only pissed her off and seemed to just make her eat more. Maybe he should shut up about that. He just couldn't help himself, it really bugged him. He wondered how he would react if he actually saw her naked again. It had been awhile.

He thought about their kids ... William Junior, appropriately nicknamed Will, being that Amy had somehow *willed* him into existence. She had never conceived when their sex life was active. When she became pregnant with him, sex was a rare commodity. At the time, Billy wondered if it had been an immaculate conception, or even if Amy had been unfaithful. Of course not, though. Amy was way too goody-two-shoes, and Will was like a little clone of Billy. Even his cowlicks were in the same places!

Two years later, she had become pregnant with Bobby, another miracle.

Since then, Amy had treated the two boys as if they were little gods. Obviously, Billy was the only screw-up in that wench's life. He could hear Amy's siren-shrill voice now, "Can't you get another job, or at least try for a promotion? ... The lawn needs to be mowed again... fix this ... fix that ... what's wrong with you ... what's wrong with you ... WHAT'S WRONG WITH YOU?!"

You, Amy-lamey are what's wrong with me. You are no longer a babe, and certainly don't satisfy me. You don't even try.

They had fought on these points a lot. She just couldn't see how she was to blame for their problems. Now Amy pretty much ignored him, unless it was to hound him about money, or the trash, or a broken something or other ... What a life. There were so many times Billy just wanted to blurt it out, hurt her to the core, but he knew it would be a death sentence. Though, to think about it, that he was so magnetic, so irresistible, that even her own sisters would betray her... besides, she would put a stop to it, and he didn't want that.

He really could *not* believe he had been getting away with this for so long.

Ginny couldn't even remember the drive home after work.

She was mad, disappointed, hurt. Why hadn't Dr. Gilmore stopped by to see her? He did have a patient on her floor, just one, but still ... shouldn't he be seeing that patient at least once per shift?

She was struggling with her apartment door key when her cell phone jingled "Super Freak", her ringtone of choice at the moment. She glanced at the caller ID. *Billy!*

"Hey!"

"Hey! Watchya doin'?"

"Just getting home from work. What about you?"

"Comin' to see you ... I've got a lollipop for you, baby."

She hesitated. "... Okay ... come on over. Hey, do you want to eat supper with me?"

"You know I can't do that. Besides, I don't have much time ..."

Yeah, yeah ... I know.

He only has time for what he wants ...

But Ginny also knew not to turn Billy down. Whenever she did, he would make himself scarce for weeks, as punishment, she guessed.

How exactly is this punishment?

There really wasn't much in this so-called relationship for her, but for some reason she found herself desperately needing Billy's attention, as pitiful as it was. When he withheld it, she felt like such a loser.

Lollipop? Lollipop my ass.

This particular sex act made her feel as though she had some power over him, although she hated it. She managed the occasional gagging sensation. He said she was the best ...

Hmmmm ... what would he do if I just... BIT IT OFF?

Oh well, she hurried into her apartment to freshen up for him.

Ginny's shifts had rotated to nights. 7 p.m. to 7 a.m. She was glad the rotations lasted eight weeks because the transition was the tough part. This time of year was the busiest, and since night shift was easier (most patients slept all night), she was glad that she was making this transition now. The onset of cold weather always brought in people with COPD exacerbations, pneumonia, and chest pain; although the chest pain patients usually went to Critical Care first, then to Telemetry. Occasionally they would trickle down to her floor, but only after they had been cleared for myocardial infarction.

Dr. Gilmore had four patients on her floor. She had seen him the other day when he was doing rounds, but he seemed to be in such a hurry that he hadn't had time to talk to her. Plus, he had this habit of charting in the patients' rooms, so he didn't spend as much time in the nurses' station as he might have been able to. It was at the end of her shift, and Ginny knew she looked frazzled. Still, they had locked eyes, and she believed that he had even winked at her! She wondered how he might extricate himself from the relationship he was currently stuck in.

So on this first evening of her night-shift rotation, Ginny walked into the nurses' station. There were six nurses on duty, including her, and thirty patients, almost their capacity. She noted on the assignment board that she had six patients, and only one of them was Dr. Gilmore's.

She greeted her coworkers. One of them, Sarah, was a permanent night nurse. She looked like a raccoon, with heavy dark bags under her eyes, but she was fairly nice.

"Hi, Ginny. Welcome back to the world of us vampires!"

Ginny smiled at her. "Yeah, I've come to suck your blooood ..."

Her attempt at humor worked as Sarah laughed. Ginny suddenly felt a surge of camaraderie. Maybe she and Sarah could become friends? Ginny had always had so much trouble fitting in.

She glanced back up at the board to see where Sarah's

assignments were located in comparison to hers; then realized that Sarah had only four patients. In fact, both of the permanent night nurses had four while Ginny and Rachel (the new kid on the block) each had six. The others had five. The happy glow she had felt momentarily was replaced by the anger that accompanies unfair treatment.

"Why do Rachel and I have bigger loads than everyone else?" Ginny demanded.

Sarah responded with an impatient sigh, "Look, Ginny, Lisa and I have taken the most difficult patients. If you want to trade with me and do the tracheostomy care on 206, that's fine with me."

"Uhhh ... no ... that's okay ..."

That stupid Rachel isn't saying a word! Just standing there, smiling and writing notes about her patients. Such a Nancy Nurse!

Ginny relented, but still felt indignation. She made some quick notes from her own patient's charts, mainly the most current orders and lab work, and then made her way into the break room to get a report from the departing shift. Man! She hated this place sometimes!

She had just finished her evening medication passes; her patients seemed to be settling in for the night. Coming out of her last patient's room, she almost ran right into Dr. John Gilmore!

"Oh! Uhhh ... hi! You're here kinda late, aren't you?" she stammered, already feeling the heat rise to her face.

"Hello, uh ... " *What is her name again?* "... Ginny! How are you tonight? Don't you work the day shift?"

Phew ... I remembered. Her name doesn't suit her, that's the problem. Ginny is a name for a down-to-earth, farm-type girl. This girl seems dark, secretive, and somewhat alarming.

But he smiled his most charming smile. Here was his chance to break the ice and maybe get rid of the discomfort this nurse made him feel.

"I work rotations. I wondered where you had been ... I mean, I haven't seen you up here much ..."

"Mmm, yes. Well uhhh … I've had such busy office hours … I don't usually do rounds till later in the evening. My patients know to expect that." *Why am I explaining myself to her?*

He certainly didn't want her to know that the discomfort she caused him had a part in the way he arranged his schedule. Besides, he liked doing things this way. It allowed him to have regular office hours, then go home and have dinner with Brenda and spend time with her before coming to the hospital to see his patients, which were still fairly few.

After his hospital rounds, he could get back home to Brenda where she'd usually be waiting up for him, reading a book and keeping their bed warm … At Burlington Hospital he made his rounds at 6 a.m.

The wretched life of a doctor; but he did love the income and the lifestyle it provided. He and Brenda were having a house built in the neighboring town of Stowe. She was overseeing the project. She was so capable!

"Well, they're all still awake, at least mine are anyway. But Mr. Smith is for sure. I just left his room."

Duh! She had nearly run him down coming out of it. Her face was turning downright purple and sweat trickled down her armpits.

"So, you work rotating shifts, do you? That must be hard. How often do you switch?" It didn't look like he was going to be able to just avoid her anymore. It was so weird for a young woman to bother him so much.

"We switch every eight weeks. It's really just the first couple of days of a new rotation that suck … I mean, are difficult."

Man! I need to watch my language. Here I am talking to an educated man and I sound like trailer-trash! Great impression!

Her mouth was so dry; she took a deep breath to try to calm herself down. She was looking as much like an idiot as she sounded.

John Gilmore smiled again. "That makes it difficult on your family, doesn't it?"

"Oh, I'm not married! Never have been. No kids. It's just me …" she babbled.

God! Now I sound like such a loser! But he IS trying to find out if I'm available, isn't he? She licked her lips and looked down at the floor, then back up at his still-smiling face.

"Well ..." he said with a slight chuckle, "... maybe we can work on that. You are certainly an attractive woman. I'm surprised somebody hasn't grabbed you up yet ..."

All right already, I need to shut up now.

He really did not know of any single men who would be interested in her, but at this moment she looked so pitiful. His words were actually more heartfelt, in a paternal sort of way, than he had originally intended. The whole conversation still felt so awkward, though.

Ginny grinned at him, unable to think of a response.

"Umm ... do you need Mr. Smith's chart?"

"No, actually I've got it right here." He tapped the chart he was holding to his chest, right in front of her face.

"Oh ... good. Okay, then ... it's been nice talking to you." She turned and started to walk self-consciously down the long hallway.

"Goodnight, Ginny."

"G'night, Dr. Gilmore," she said, turning her head to look back at him.

Now what was THAT all about? It almost sounded like he wanted to fix me up with someone. Maybe he had to make it sound that way because of his girlfriend, or fiancé, or whatever she is.

There was no doubt in Ginny's mind that he was interested in her. He was just being kind of cryptic about it. He had smiled at her so ...

"Ginny!"

Yowza! She jerked her head toward the nurses' station. Sarah and Lisa were sitting there, a magazine in front of each of them.

"216 just called out. She needs to use the bathroom."

"Yeah, okay ... thanks."

Thanks for nothing you lazy cow, thought Ginny bitterly.

Ginny slid into her freezing car and yanked the door shut, pulling in a blast of cold air into her face. Her nose was running and her eyes were watering. She absentmindedly wiped her nose on the sleeve of her sheepskin suede jacket. She looked at the smear she had created and rubbed at it with her mitten.

Damn! This is a $200 coat!

She had bought it with the upcoming holidays in mind. Everyone, including Billy, would gather at Mom's house for the event of FOOD, her mom's cure for any and all problems. Ginny might be able to talk Billy into going for a walk with her, which would give her a chance to show off how she looked in this great coat. It wasn't unusual to take walks after dinner at Mom's. The graveyard was only a few blocks away, and they often went to visit Dad's grave.

It was something to do, and an excuse to get them out of the stiflingly close proximity of each other. Too often these family gatherings, if you wanted to call it that, turned into arguments. She and her sisters just didn't get along. Amy acted so 'superior than thou' (if only she knew), and Cassie—Jesus, Cassie was like a freak of nature! Mom would always just get upset and go cry in her room, until they'd all feel bad and coax her out, pretending that they were all okay with each other. Thank God the holidays were far and few between.

Damn it was cold!

Her car sputtered to life and she slowly pulled out of the hospital parking lot.

She had only heard from Billy once since Halloween, the last time he had come over. He had looked so depressed and had been a total ass. All they did was to get completely wasted and watch *Nightmare on Elm Street.* Since then she'd only received a brief email: "Work's gotten crazy. I'm way behind. Me and Amy have been at each other's throats. I'll call you when things settle down."

It had been almost three weeks! Their affair had always been this way: hot, then cold. She used to get so hurt by his silence;

now she was just used to it. That didn't mean she wasn't annoyed by it.

What is he up to?

She knew that if she said something, or God forbid, let him know she was upset, Billy would stay away even longer.

When is this charade going to end? We are such a better couple than Amy and him. Can't he see that?

He kept saying that the boys needed to be older and more independent before he left. Ginny thought of her two nephews. She really did love them, especially Bobby. He was such a little clown. They both were extraordinarily cute, with their big brown eyes … they looked just like Billy!

Well, it might not matter much longer anyway!

Dr. Gilmore … John … she thought fondly, *is definitely interested in me. He said he was surprised that nobody had grabbed me up yet. His intent that he would be the one to do so was obvious. He had such a twinkle in his eye when he said it! He even said that they'd have to work on my marital status. If that wasn't a hint … He called me attractive—or did he say beautiful?* Ginny was sure that he had to watch what he said inside the hospital in case anyone overheard him. But she fully understood the body language and unspoken words.

Billy would be sorry one day when she was living the life of a doctor's wife, driving a Porsche, spending her days at the spa … she would totally blow him off then, and not in the way he liked either.

Ginny couldn't wait to get home and get to bed. She actually slept better during the day.

Maybe I really am a vampire!

Janice took refuge and comfort in her visits with Beverly. They had been friends for years, having met at the hospital when their respective husbands, Chuck and Jim, were both dying of lung cancer. The women had confided in each other their anger regarding the cigarette addictions of their spouses, feeling that they'd had only themselves to blame for their untimely demises. Neither of the women had enjoyed blissful marriages; they had a lot to commiserate about. The only difference was that Beverly had no children, thus she vicariously lived through Janice as she talked about the escapades of Amy, Cassie, and Ginny.

The friends usually met at Beverly's house, due to Cassie's unpredictable moods. They would drink coffee, play cribbage, reminisce about their husbands, and Beverly would give Janice impractical advice about how to handle her daughters' problems. It was sweet, but how could she know, not having children of her own? It did help Janice to be able to talk to someone who was such a good listener, though.

When the weather was nice, they would take long walks two to three times a week, and during the colder months, Wednesday evenings were their standing date. The hours seemed to fly by when she and Beverly got to talking.

So it was on the occasional Wednesday evening that Billy found himself "working late" and making the drive to Janice's for some *really* kinky sex with … Cassie.

She would do anything he asked. Granted, she wasn't all that easy to look at, but she didn't seem to mind at all when he stuck his face in a *Penthouse* as he invaded her "backdoor". This was something that Ginny absolutely didn't like, and Amy … well, he never even asked her. She had always been a strictly by-the-book missionary-position type of gal.

Billy didn't even have to part with any of his precious dope. Cassie was a freebie! The poor girl was absolutely in love with Billy and worshipped the ground he walked on. Unlike Ginny,

Cassie required no promises of any kind. Billy amazed himself at the power he had over the sisters. Of course, with Ginny, it had started when she was still pretty much an adolescent. It had been quite easy because she had idolized him so. He treated her like a kid sister in public, and nobody had ever been the wiser. Even now, everyone just thought of their relationship as "sweet".

Crazy, man!

He had never even considered Cassie in this way, until a few months ago when he had left his favorite baseball cap at Janice's. He, Amy, and the boys had eaten dinner there the previous Sunday. He had driven over on a Wednesday after work, wanting his hat for a game he had tickets for the next evening. He had had an active afternoon on the Internet, and was all worked up. When he arrived at Janice's and found Cassie home alone, he had thought, *why not*? She had been very willing. He told Cassie he would come back as long as she never, ever told a living soul. She had sworn to secrecy, and he knew that the threat of not having his attention was enough to keep her quiet.

Sometimes Billy wondered about his own sanity. It would've been one thing to have an affair with a stranger and have Amy find out about it—but with her very own SISTERS? What?? Was he nuts!? Well ... Amy deserved it. She treated him like a second-class citizen. She didn't appreciate how hard he worked. She was so quick to point out his faults, or at least what *she* considered to be faults. He really had very few, if any, as far as he was concerned. Amy just didn't know how to be a wife. All she cared about were the boys, and herself of course. If Amy ever found out about any of this, he honestly didn't know what she would do. But he knew it would be bad, whatever it was. So why did he take the chance? Especially with *Cassie*? There was just something about it, like he was getting away with a major bank robbery or something. It was hard to explain ... he couldn't help himself ...

It was the weekend and John was not on call. He and his partner from the Burlington office took turns with this ball-and-chain responsibility, with the exception of any of their patients admitted to Mercy. John had given his long-term partner and friend, George, the option to be involved with his new office in the small town of Adamant, but George had not wanted to travel even this fairly short distance.

Mercy was located in Montpelier, but there were several small towns just north of this capital city from which to draw patients. Even though Montpelier was the capital of Vermont, it too was pretty darned small. John's new practice was slowly growing, but so many of these Northerners were tough old birds, denying any need for a doctor's care, or frankly, just not trusting it. Needless to say, most of this new clientele was made up of elderly widows.

So on this weekend, George had Burlington under control, and John had no patients currently admitted to Mercy. He was free! But what to do? He wasn't even sure why he was wondering about that as he opened his eyes early Saturday morning. He was sure that Brenda had a full agenda. She had learned to take full advantage of any free time he had.

She was used to his early morning hours, and responded to his stirrings by moving closer, draping her arm across his belly and her leg over both of his. She nuzzled his neck and he turned his face into her hair to breathe in the scent of her—a warm, sleepy fragrance, both familiar and comforting. Sex was not a priority in their relationship, not that they didn't have an active sex life, and they certainly felt passionately about each other, but they shared something much deeper. Sometimes just lying there all tangled up in each other was enough. He felt an overwhelming contentment just having her by his side. She was his best friend, his confidante, and his cheerleader when he started to feel insecure or worried about opening the new office. In a way, she was also his business partner. She acted as receptionist during their business hours two days a week, plus she handled all the finances. He trusted her implicitly.

"How about you get some coffee and the newspaper? Let's read it right here in bed," she whispered in his ear.

"Hmm ... how about *you* get some coffee and—"

"John!" She snuck her fingers into his armpit and tickled him.

"No! No! Please ... stop! Okay, okay, you lazy bum. Just keep the bed warm ..." as he kissed her forehead and trapped her hand in his own. "I love you, sweetie. I'll be right back."

He reluctantly slid out from under the deluxe featherbed that kept the chill far from their slumbering bodies. His bare feet hit the cold wood floor of the little rental house in which they temporarily resided while their new home was being built. For a rental, this was not a bad place. Living in Adamant was like living in what everyone would consider the typical, quaint New England village. The tiny town boasted a handful of specialty shops, boutiques, a phenomenal bakery/deli, and a mom-and-pop Italian restaurant that would rival anything a big city like Boston might offer. It wasn't a posh place, but warm and inviting, with everything made fresh from scratch by an authentic Italian family named Bolotto. What was really nice was that it was all within walking distance from their humble abode.

John decided to surprise Brenda. He put on a jogging suit and trotted over to the bakery for some fresh-out-of-the-oven onion bagels, homemade cream cheese with chives, and two large Café Mochas with extra shots of hazelnut. He picked up the paper from the front porch as he made his way back into the house. Brenda was ready. She had placed their reading pillows against the headboard and had brought their breakfast-in-bed tray in from the kitchen.

He swore, she could just read his mind!

Thanksgiving came with the usual chaos. The Miller family managed to get along until about halfway through the meal, which was a shame, because it was so delicious. And Mom had spent hours preparing it. Amy and Ginny had both done their small parts.

Of course, Cassie hadn't done squat.

Amy had made cranberry sauce from fresh cranberries, as well as homemade pumpkin pie. Ginny's assignment was mashed potatoes. The potatoes were obviously flaked, dried potatoes from a box and hadn't traveled well. They had no business being topped by Mom's rich, creamy gravy.

Amy just couldn't help herself …

"Ginny, you *do* know how to peel and boil real potatoes, don't you? This is Thanksgiving, for God's sake."

"Jesus, Amy! I guess if all I had was a part-time job in a stupid bookstore, like you, instead of a back-breaking full-time job as a nurse, maybe I'd have time to peel and boil potatoes … you are such a bitch!"

"Now, girls. The potatoes are fine. I can't even tell the difference. Let's just enjoy our meal and be grateful for all that we have … please?" Mom pleaded.

Everyone got quiet but a dark cloud hovered over their heads as they finished eating; and then, one by one they made their way into the living room, leaving Amy and Mom at the table.

"Amy, what on earth is the matter? Why do you constantly feel the need to put Ginny down?"

"God, Mum. I don't know. She just really irks me, and I do not understand why you don't make Cassie pull her weight around here …"

"We've talked about that, Amy. You know what a mess she makes of everything. She just isn't blessed with your capability. She has had such a tough time of it—" Janice whispered.

"Mom! She has *created* her own disasters, one after the other.

Are you saying she's not responsible for her 'mistakes' as you would like to think of them?" Amy whispered fiercely back.

"Now is not the time or place—"

"It's *never* the time or place!"

Janice put her forehead down over her crossed hands. Amy couldn't tell if she was praying or what.

"Look, Mom. I'm really sorry. This was a wonderful dinner, really. Everything was just so perfect. The potatoes ... they just set me off. I'm sorry."

Janice looked up at Amy with teary eyes and placed one of her hands over Amy's.

"It's okay, honey. I understand. Just please try to be more forgiving."

"I will, Mum ... I guess I'm just really frustrated with Billy too."

At that moment, Billy, Cassie, and Ginny entered the room, leaving the boys in the living room to watch a parade on TV.

"What are you guys talking about?" Ginny demanded.

"Nothing, really, nothing Ginny. I'm sorry about what I said about the potatoes. They were fine—honestly."

"I *know* they were fine," Ginny retorted. "*I'm* going for a walk. Anyone want to come?" she asked, knowing full well that her snappy response to Amy's apology would count HER out for a walk.

Billy hesitated as Ginny looked expectantly at him, then said, "Yeah, I suppose some fresh air would be good after pigging out on such great food ..."

Cassie chose that moment to storm out of the room, slamming her bedroom door after entering it with a huff.

"What's *her* problem?" Billy asked snidely. "God knows, if anyone could use the exercise ..."

"Well, I guess she doesn't want to go. Come on then, Billy."

The two of them donned their coats and made their way outside.

As the front door shut behind them, Amy turned to her mother. "Mom ..."

"Amy, I don't want to talk about Ginny or Cassie. Besides, Cassie can probably hear us through the door…" Mom whispered.

Cassie's room was just off the kitchen, in Dad's old study-slash-library.

"No, no. I don't want to talk about them anyway …"

They sat in silence for a few minutes; then both stood and started to clear the table.

Amy wasn't sure how to begin. Mom had this idea in her head that Amy's life was so perfect. She sat back down.

"Mom …" she started again.

"Oh, don't worry, honey. You go lie down and get some rest. I'll get these dishes done. It's easier for me to just do it myself."

"No, Mom. Can't I talk to you?"

Janice stopped gathering plates and sat down.

"I'm thinking about divorcing Billy."

"*What?* Amy! You can't do that … think of Will and Bobby."

"I do, Ma … every day. Billy and I have really grown apart. We can't even have a mundane conversation without it turning into World War III."

"Amy, nobody ever said that marriage was easy. But it's for life, for better or worse, in sickness and in health … even the Justice of the Peace said those words, didn't he?"

"I swear, Mom, you don't understand. You don't see the side of Billy that I see every day. He's *mean*! You just heard what he said about Cassie. Plus, he's lazy, and he hates me."

"He doesn't hate you, Amy. Billy had a very rough childhood, losing both of his parents at such a young age—"

"I AM SICK TO DEATH OF HEARING THAT SOB STORY!"

"Ssshhhh, Amy!"

"No! I won't *sshhhh*! I don't know why you think I have it so easy. I am miserable, Mom. MISERABLE! Sometimes I just wish he would *die* so I could at least get his life insurance money and be *happy* for once in my life! For crying out loud, HE'S *WORTH MORE DEAD* to me than he is alive!"

Janice just looked at her daughter, open-mouthed and stunned at Amy's outburst. "Amy … why don't the two of you go to counseling or something?"

"*Counseling*? Why didn't you and Dad go to *counseling*? If anyone ever needed it, you two did! Why did you stay in that God-forsaken marriage, Mom? I will tell you this, I WILL NOT BE LIKE YOU!"

And with that, she ran down the hall, up the stairs, and into her old room, still preserved from when she was growing up in that house. It brought her no comfort whatsoever.

Janice robotically resumed clearing the table, as she had done countless times before.

Cassie sat by her closed door; she'd heard every word. How dare Billy say something about her weight? And that comment about 'pigging out' while looking right at her? And how could he just take off and go for a walk with Ginny? He should have insisted that Cassie go along! Cassie hated her sisters more than anything.

And she was starting to hate Billy too.

Ginny and Billy walked side by side, but each held their coat collars close around their necks and ears to ward off the biting wind.

"It's cold as shit."

"No kidding; but it's even colder in that damned house," Ginny muttered.

They continued to walk in silence.

"Do you want to go back?"

"To what, Billy? Do you want to go back so you can be with your *sweet, loving wife*?"

They continued to walk in an even heavier silence.

"What the fuck is wrong with you?"

Ginny ignored the question and strode ahead, leaving Billy behind.

He jogged to catch up.

"Ginny ... *Jesum Crow.*"

"*What*, Billy?!"

They were arriving at the graveyard.

"Okay, *fine*. Let's just go back."

"Ginny, what's wrong with you? Are you actually mad at me for being busy at work?"

"I don't know, Billy. I don't think you have any intention of ever leaving Amy, and you're just too chicken-shit to admit it! You are ruining my life! Besides, someone else is very interested in me. A *doctor* at the hospital."

"What? Who?'

"None of your damned business."

They turned around and started to head back toward Mom's house; now the wind was at their backs.

"Ginny, there's nobody else and you know it. Just like there's nobody else for me."

Ginny glared at him out of the corner of her eye while trying to keep her head aimed straight ahead.

He caught her look and started to laugh.

She kept a poker face for as long as she could before she cracked a smile.

"I hate you," she said.

"I know. I hate you too."

They managed another block as their ears and noses started to become prickly numb with the cold.

"Don't you like my new coat?" Ginny sniffled.

"Yeah. Yeah, it's a great coat, and it looks great on you. But it would look better off ..."

Ginny rolled her eyes.

They continued in oppressive silence.

When they entered the stifling heat of Mom's house, Billy collected his family and headed home.

~

Billy clomped up the long flight of stairs to the office of Dr. Patricia Hurt, his faithful shrink. She happened to be employed by the insurance company. Either the company truly cared about the well-being of its employees, or they wanted to have access to the personal information that might be revealed should an employee seek the free psychological assistance that was offered. Billy didn't care. Honest to God, he didn't even care if he was fired from his stupid job.

Dr. Hurt, who insisted that her patients call her Patty, seemed to need emotional help of her own. What a name! Dr. Hurt! No wonder she had her patients call her Patty.

Patty was like putty in Billy's hands.

The door squeaked open on its rusty hinges; Billy plopped down on the worn, tweed-covered couch in the waiting room.

The door to Patty's private office was ajar. She quickly filled the doorframe, telling Billy to "Come on in, for gosh sakes!"

She had a perpetual blush that blended into her carrot-topped head.

Patty was nice and accommodating.

She supplied Billy with his anti-depressants, his anti-anxiety meds, and an ear to listen to his never-ending complaints about getting the short end of the stick of life.

She rustled some of the papers on her desk and then looked up at him.

"Let's talk about … your mother today."

"You have *got* to be kidding, Patty."

"No, Billy. I'm not. You really have some unresolved issues. You are going to have to deal with them someday, why not today?"

Billy's mother had died in a car accident when Billy was eleven years old. She had been drinking. Heavily. In fact, she had never *stopped* drinking since the day that Billy's dad had fled the scene almost three years earlier. The wreck had put an end to all that.

Billy and his mom had moved in with his grandmother shortly after his dad disappeared, and Billy had stayed there after the death of his mother. There were hints that physical abuse had occurred at the hands of his grandmother. She had been an angry woman.

Patty was convinced that Billy held some deep-seeded anger at his mother for 'abandoning' him, even though it was actually his father who had done so.

Billy was quite certain that he felt nothing toward his dead mother, nor toward his good-for-nothing father, who ended up dying of liver cirrhosis a few years later.

You would've thought that after his mother died, his Dad would have come for him. But no, Billy ended up living with an old woman who made no secret about the fact that she hadn't wanted him there.

"My mother ... Okay... alright... what do you want to know?"

"Oh, Billy, do we have to dance this dance again?"

Billy snorted.

She fixed her gaze on him, willing him to air his dirty laundry.

The waiting felt like an eternity.

"Yeah, well ... I don't know why she had to go and kill herself like that. Was I such an awful kid?"

There! Was that what Peppermint Patty wanted to hear?

"Billy, you know it was just an accident."

"But it happened because she was drunk. I swear, she must've hated me ..." Billy let his eyes get watery before he looked up at Patty with a pained expression.

"I just ... can't ... talk about it." he whispered hoarsely.

She mustered a look of pity, although she truly felt frustrated that she was unable to get anywhere with Billy. With his history, he was a walking psychologist's dream. If she could only break through. Was she capable enough in her field? Sometimes she really didn't feel like she knew what she was doing ... but she had gone to school for this! Many years of education! Surely she could help this troubled man.

"Okay, Billy. What do you want to talk about today?"

"Well, I'm glad you asked. I'm having a lot of trouble sleeping ... I'm thinking Ambien might help."

Patty hesitated, sighed, and reached for her prescription pad.

"Hey, beautiful!"

Amy was not accustomed to being addressed in this way; so it was several seconds before she looked up from alphabetizing the new fiction that had just come in.

"Oh, Geoffrey! Hi!" She fumbled with the box in front of her.

Geoffrey was a new employee at the bookstore. He was a junior at Burlington College, where Amy had attended. He was a literature major, as Amy had been. He was also pretty darned cute, in an Al Pacino sort of way. Although he flirted with Amy, he didn't seem quite comfortable in his own skin. It was as though he didn't really know how to flirt and was just trying it on for size. For this reason, Amy didn't mind the flirtation. She could tell he sincerely liked her and she was completely flattered. His obvious discomfort made her feel kind of protective of him. His apparent nervousness also allowed her to feel a confidence that she didn't normally feel.

"So, what are we working on?"

Amy smiled at him and said, "Well, *you* are now working on finishing up the alphabetizing and shelving of this new fiction. It's about time for me to go and pick up the boys."

She looked down at her watch. "Oh! It's only two-thirty! You're a little early, aren't you?"

"Yeah ... but I haven't clocked in yet. I'll wait till closer to three ... just had some time on my hands ..."

She looked into his dark eyes, almost hidden under his thick, floppy hair, which he flung over to the side with a quick flick of his head. It was so shiny and smooth that it fell right back into place over his eyes. He blinked at her and smiled a crooked, sheepish grin.

Something inside of her tingled.

~

With the exception of the disaster that was Thanksgiving, Ginny hadn't heard from Billy since Halloween. She was sick to death of the way he treated her. Of course, she knew she was partly to blame for that. After all, she had been at his beck and call for years. Every time he slightly crooked his little finger, she came running. She hated the waiting.

What am I waiting for? A few short minutes of his precious time?

She wondered if it was just because his wife happened to be her sister that she was able to have been so patient all these years. She had never intended to hurt Amy; at least she didn't think so....

Her feelings toward Billy were changing. She was sure that her hope for a future with John had something to do with that. Maybe fate had played a hand in this somehow. Maybe Billy had only been a diversion all these years to keep her free for when John came into her life. It was easy for Ginny to imagine being the wife of a doctor. She had no problem spending money, especially on herself. Being Mrs. John Gilmore would afford her some of the luxuries she not only desired, but deserved! So far, this life hadn't cut her such a sweet deal. Billy had caused her enough heartbreak to last a lifetime. But no more!

As if on cue, her cell phone rang.

"Hello?"

"Hi, Baby."

"Who is this?"

"Whaddya mean, who is this?"

"John, is that you, sweetie?"

"John? Who's John?"

"Oh ... I'm sorry. It's *you*, Billy."

"Yeah, it's me. Jesus, Ginny. You do have caller ID. And you certainly know my voice. Who the hell is John?"

"That's really none of your business."

"Goddammit, Ginny! Stop trying to make me jealous. It's pretty obvious what you're trying to do."

"Billy, I don't need to play games with you, the way that *you* have played games with me all these years. I'm past you, in case you haven't noticed. Waaay past you."

"Fuck you, Ginny." He hung up with a loud click.

"Fuck you too, Billy."

And as her finger pressed the end button, a flood of emotions engulfed her. A shuddering sob erupted from the depths of her soul.

~

Ginny trudged down A-wing. For once her patients were in the same general area. Nursing was hard enough without all the extra walking required when assignments were split between two or more wings.

The halls were decorated for the holidays. There were Christmas trees that had empty but festively wrapped boxes underneath, and assorted paper wreaths and stockings taped to the walls.

Is this supposed to be cheerful? Who would possibly feel cheerful while stuck in a hospital?

Ginny didn't really believe in Christmas anyway.

But as she turned to enter room 224, where she had been summoned to assist a patient to the commode, her peripheral vision caught a glimpse of a figure very recognizable to her.

Dr. Gilmore!

Something was different. She turned to look where he was standing at the nurses' station. He was wearing a Santa hat.

How cute!

He was holding something over his head as he stood there. Ginny watched as two nurses clumsily filed out from behind the desk and tentatively kissed his offered cheek. Dr. Gilmore was chuckling and the nurses were giggling as they returned rather quickly to their stations. Ginny then realized that what he had held over his head was mistletoe.

As he started to turn in her direction, she yanked the door open without knocking, and rushed into the patient's room. She was practically hyperventilating.

The patient looked up at her quizzically. Ginny rushed into his bathroom and called out, "I just have to wash my hands." She ran the water until she was able to compose herself.

She hadn't seen John Gilmore since the humiliating conversation just before Thanksgiving. In truth, she had been pissed.

Is he avoiding me? Or is he just as embarrassed as I am about the intense attraction between us? Maybe he's still trying to work out his relationship thing? I really should give him the benefit of the doubt ...

Ginny considered the two nurses who had just kissed him. Neither was attractive.

Why would he have brought in that mistletoe? Is it just an excuse to get a kiss from me? Of course it is!

She looked at herself in the small, square mirror above the sink. She was a little flushed, but it looked good on her. Hell, she really did look pretty good tonight!

She stepped out of the bathroom.

"I was just checking to see if you needed anything before you went to sleep," she said to the frail, elderly gentleman lying in the bed.

"Well … that's why I called," he said, "because I need to use the bathroom."

"Oh, yeah."

She walked over to his bedside and helped him as he very slowly and gingerly made his way to a sitting position on the side of the bed. Finally, he stood on wobbly legs before beginning the painful shuffle to the bathroom. Ginny held his arm.

"Stop rushing me!" he said.

She realized that she had been tugging on his arm in the direction of the bathroom.

"Oh. I'm sorry." She made a concentrated effort to allow him to lead the way, while just providing physical support so he didn't fall flat on the floor and break a hip or something.

Old people, she thought. *This old geezer is just trying to milk the medical system for all it's worth! He's probably indigent.*

She smiled politely at him.

When he was finally finished, Ginny practically ran out of the room and down the hall.

Dr. Gilmore had only one patient on the floor this evening, and even though it was not one of hers, Ginny knew the room number. She quickly scanned the hallway for any sign of him.

"Looking for someone, Ginny?"

"Umm … no …"

"Dr. Gilmore was just here. He asked if you were working. You should have seen him. Dressed like Santa and giving out kisses of all things."

"Oh! Uhhh … I needed to ask him something … about a patient I had last week …"

"Well, you could probably catch him. He just walked through the door into the stairwell."

"Really?" Ginny impulsively ran to the stairwell door. As she opened it, she could hear his footsteps on the landing on the floor below.

"Dr. Gilmore!"

The footsteps stopped.

"Yes?"

She clattered down the steps to the landing where he stood, and then realized that she had absolutely nothing to say.

"Uhhh … Merry Christmas!" she said, her smile twitching.

Christmas was still two weeks away.

"Well … thank you. Same to you and your family." He looked terrified as he attempted to smile back at her.

"I saw that you had some mistletoe …"

Oh my God! I can't believe I just said that!

He wasn't sure what he should do.

He slowly pulled it out of his lab coat pocket and hesitantly held it up over his head.

What had he been thinking to have brought this thing in here?

He offered his cheek, as he had with the others, but Ginny circumvented the maneuver and planted a wet one smack dab on his lips.

All of a sudden the stairwell felt stiflingly hot and seemed to be closing in on them. He caught a whiff of her breath. *Sour.* And her body odor. *Peeuuw.* She was obviously sweating. He felt repulsed and abruptly turned, practically running down the stairs. *SHIT*!

Ginny was momentarily stunned by her own actions. She felt the heat from her neck and face, and the beads of sweat on her forehead and upper lip. Shaking, she turned and walked back up the stairs. When she entered the unit back through that fateful door, she noticed Lisa and Sarah exchanging knowing looks.

Christmas was nothing more than just another day. It came, and it went. Ginny was thoroughly depressed. She was scheduled to work the holiday, and was grateful for the excuse to not have to go to Mom's. As it turned out, Cassie was sick with a bad head cold, so Mom had just gone to Amy and Billy's for dinner and to exchange gifts.

Very uneventful, which was better than the usual.

Ginny made her rounds on the following Tuesday evening to exchange her own gifts with them. When she stopped by Billy and Amy's, Billy was already asleep, or so Amy said. They had gotten Ginny a calendar. She gave them her gift of specialty coffee beans.

Gifting had never been an extravagant gesture between any of them. Mom always gave money in a card. She didn't like shopping in crowds.

Another year almost gone, and what did Ginny have to show for it?

She was utterly confused about John. He *had* kissed her back. Of that she was sure. But then he had run off like Cinderella at the stroke of midnight! Was he playing games with her or what? He was the one who had brought the mistletoe in, just *begging* for a kiss from her ... She had seen him a couple of times since, but it had been at a distance. He had smiled and waved, but acted as though nothing had passed between them. She really needed to get to the bottom of all this.

That man was going to have to make a decision. And soon.

Billy woke up in a sweat. The dream, or nightmare, was already becoming vague. Something about getting caught red-handed by Amy with *both* Cassie and Ginny. He seemed to remember the dream taking place at Burkette Falls. The dream part had been the threesome that he had been thoroughly enjoying. Billy actually still had a bit of an erection. The nightmare part had been Amy showing up, screeching like a banshee.

He reached down under the blankets and fondled himself and tried to imagine being back in the dream. It didn't take long. His imagination could be very vivid when he wanted it to be.

Afterward, he sleepily reminisced about the countless afternoons he and Ginny had spent at the falls. For the longest time, it had been their special place. The only place really, that they could go when Ginny was still living with her parents. After she moved out on her own, it was easier to use Ginny's apartment. But, whenever he felt that Ginny was beginning to slip away from him, he had made arrangements to meet her back at the falls, sometimes with a bottle of wine, sometimes with a small gift ... it didn't take much to make her happy.

He was starting to sense that Ginny was becoming agitated again. He knew it would pass. He no longer worried about Ginny telling Amy anything. At this point, she was just as guilty as he was. Cassie was another story. He had not been to see her for quite awhile; frankly, he didn't really have the urge to continue with that, as easy as it was.

He actually cringed when he thought of Cassie. Well, so far she had kept her mouth shut.

So far, so good.

John and Brenda were sound asleep when the telephone pierced the darkness at 2 a.m. Brenda fumbled for the receiver.

"Hello?"

"Hi … yeah … this is Virginia calling … from Mercy. Is Dr. Gilmore in?"

"Yes, he's right here. Hold on." She jostled John as she handed him the phone. "It's the hospital."

John put the receiver to his ear. *Wow!* This was his first callback from Mercy since he had started his practice there.

"This is Dr. Gilmore," he said.

"Oh, Dr. Gilmore. I'm sorry to wake you. Your patient in 217, Mrs. Simoneaux, may have had a heart attack. They are doing a 12-lead on her right now," Ginny said in her most professional voice.

"I'll be right there."

When he arrived fifteen minutes later, all was rather quiet. Ginny approached him. There was something challenging in her demeanor.

"It's okay now. She's asleep. The 12-lead showed no changes, and her first set of labs were negative. Like I said, she's already back to sleep … but we did put oxygen and a monitor on her for the night," she said smugly.

"What?" he asked. "You're the one who called me?"

"Of course, she's my patient tonight."

He walked around Ginny as she stared intently at him. He shuffled through the charts until he located 217.

"The lab results and the EKG are right there in the chart," she said with a smile. But there was question in her eyes, a question he not only didn't want to hear but did not want to answer.

"Thanks, Ginny." He sighed as he turned in the direction of room 217.

"But she's asleep!"

He glanced back at her.

What? Does she think she can call me in for a patient who might have had a heart attack, and then I'm not even going to SEE the patient? Something doesn't feel right about this.

He knocked on the door and entered the room, careful to hit the light switch for the dimmer light behind the bed, rather than the bright overheads.

Mrs. Simoneaux roused from her sleep and blinked up at him. She reached for her glasses on the bedside table and perched them on the tip of her little nose.

"Why, Dr. Gilmore! What are you doing here? I'm fine …just fine … really I am. I just had a little spell is all."

"What do you mean, 'a little spell'? Tell me exactly what happened," he gently inquired.

"Oh, it's silly, really. No need to fuss. My nurse was in here, checking on me, and knocked over the wastepaper basket in the dark. I didn't know it was her at first; so of course, I panicked! You know how I panic! Ginny was very worried about me and wanted to check my heart, since it was beating so, and my breathing and all … you know how it is when I panic. But she had me all checked out anyway … and I'm A-okay!"

John stared down at her, dumbfounded. "Did you actually have any chest pain, Mrs. Simoneaux?"

"Oh, no. Nothing like that … just my usual anxious spell, you know."

"Yes … well then… as long as I'm here, let *me* check you out."

He took his stethoscope from around his neck, listened to her heart, lungs, checked her pulse, and looked at the tests, which indeed, had been done.

"I'm so glad this seems to have been a false alarm, Mrs. Simoneaux. But let's keep this monitor on you until morning, to make sure."

"Can I take off this awful oxygen?"

"In the morning, as long as all stays well. I'll see you then, dear."

"Okay. Goodnight, Dr. Gilmore. See you very soon, I suppose."

"Yes, very soon."

He smiled reassuringly at the patient, turned the light back off, and then left the room.

He was livid that this poor woman had just undergone what must have been frightful for her, getting jabbed with a needle for her blood, the sticky tabs all over her body for the 12-lead...plus the fear that something dreadful might be wrong with her. All because of a panic attack induced by the stupidity of this nurse ... not to mention that her panic attacks were both frequent and clearly marked in her chart ...

He stalked up to the nurses' station.

"Ginny, just what made you think that Mrs. Simoneaux was having a heart attack?"

"She was short of breath and said that her chest felt funny. Didn't I do the right thing?" she asked, all wide-eyed and innocent.

What could he say?

He took a deep breath before responding.

"Of course you did ... of course you did. I'll be back in the morning."

Ginny spoke to his back as he walked away from her.

"I'm really glad I was there for her. And you know, better safe than sorry ..."

Right. Better safe than sorry.

John really had no reason to think that Ginny might be harassing him.

The call in the middle of the night was probably legitimate. She had followed protocol by receiving orders from the Hospitalist, and then notifying me … It was just that moronic kiss in the stairwell!

Why? *Why* had he done that?! *She* was the one who had kissed *him*. But he was the one who had brought in that ridiculous mistletoe.

AAAGGGGHHHH!

He was just going to have to watch her … and watch himself. He did not want to be accused of impropriety.

How on earth am I going to handle her? Jesus, why do I even have to 'handle' her at all? How did I get into this mess? Trying to be a nice guy, that's how. Damn it.

Maybe he was worried for no reason.

I practically invited the kiss by having the mistletoe. But I had not intended that … not at all! She is one screwy and strange girl. And she looks so sleazy!

He had Brenda, and was quite happy with her.

Brenda … Christ! I would never do anything to betray her trust. What is this girl up to? Is she even up to anything? Am I being self-important to think that she is? Maybe it's all in my head. Jesus! What should I do?

Nothing. That's what I'll do.

After all, there was nothing *to* do.

Ginny burst into tears the second she got into her car. He had actually acted angrily toward her! Here she was, taking extra-special care of his patients, and he practically yelled at her!

Why had he acted that way? You'd think he would have been glad that she came up with the idea of calling him in. *Doesn't he GET it? This is the perfect way for him to get out and see her. Is it possible he doesn't get it?*

Mrs. Simoneaux had certainly done her part well by responding exactly as Ginny had anticipated when she knocked over the trash can in the dark room. It had been so perfect—except for John Gilmore's reaction.

What was wrong with that man? Maybe he was just plain exhausted, and not acting himself.

Ginny thought about this for a few minutes.

Well, that certainly makes sense ... the poor guy.

Ginny had totally forgotten that he had been up all day seeing patients.

He was simply tired and not thinking clearly. Once he thinks about it, he'll realize the opportunity I laid out for him. He was just way too tired to get it, that's all.

She felt better already.

Amy was losing weight. She was feeling good these days. She had been walking in the mall three mornings each week after dropping the boys off at school. She would've done it every morning but on Tuesdays and Thursdays she was taking a little more time getting ready for work. Those were the days Geoffrey worked. She wanted to look and smell fresh—not that she smelled bad on Mondays, Wednesdays, and Fridays ...

Although his shift didn't start until three, it seemed Geoffrey was showing up earlier and earlier; yet he didn't clock in until three. What was that all about? *Hmmm* ...

They talked about books. Books they loved. Books they hated. Books that were boring, but they'd finished anyway. Books that were so great they had read them twice or more!

Their tastes were so similar. It was getting easier to talk with him all the time. And he seemed much more comfortable as well.

Amy hadn't felt this good in such a long time. It seemed as though she was just living for Tuesdays and Thursdays, looking forward to them, figuring out what to wear ...

She had even been late picking up the boys from school a couple times! Time flew by when she was talking with Geoffrey.

But that's all it was—just talking. About books.

After all, he was practically a kid. She still didn't know much about him personally. Probably never would. But this new friendship was making her life almost fun. She was more *alive.*

She found herself pouring over the bookshelves that lined their living room wall, looking for old books that she had read like they were long-lost friends.

Unfortunately, Amy found herself to be more and more irritated with Billy all the time. When she thought about it, she realized they had *nothing* in common. They never really had. What on earth had attracted her to Billy in the first place?

Mom was going to kill her, but Amy *was* going to divorce him. It was only a matter of time. Mom might believe in "till death do us part", but this marriage was like a slow and painful death itself.

If only Amy could have set aside more than that paltry $25 a week. She simply didn't make that much money and she did not want to make her withholding obvious.

Billy had access to the checkbook. Since his pay was direct deposit and varied according to his so-called productivity (more like, what he was able to save his skin-flint employer), and hers were regular paychecks she had to deposit, he would be able to see if these deposits became even more measly than they already were.

Amy was so meticulous about paying the bills and keeping a ledger, she had made it virtually impossible to hide any significant amount of money.

She had taken it out and counted her stash the other day—$3,900. Almost four grand!

It was a lot of money to her, although she knew it wouldn't go far. Of course, she'd probably get child support, but she would more than likely have to fight for it every month. Could she get Billy's wages garnished?

She wasn't sure how all this divorce-business worked, but she'd look into it.

Twenty Years Earlier

How exciting college life was! The sense of freedom was exhilarating. At first having a roommate was a bit daunting for Amy, especially one as pretty as Ada; but after a few weeks they had settled into a comfortable sisterly relationship, thankfully without all the baggage and history.

Amy didn't spend much time in her dorm room anyway. Her classes started early and she often spent evenings in the sprawling campus library.

Ada was a typical college coed. She was hoping to be inducted into a sorority, and was always ready for a party, anytime, anywhere.

This was just not Amy's way.

Ada laughed at Amy's serious personality, and as hard as she tried to get Amy to let her hair down once in a while, she just as easily, but good-naturedly, gave up. So the two lived together but had very separate lives. It worked.

Amy was the kind of girl who didn't really fit into any particular crowd. She was well-liked by almost everyone and she would flit in and out of the different types of crowds with some degree of comfort, but without getting too close. Amy's mode of operation was to always be interested in what the other person had to say, while revealing very little about herself.

She felt it important to be liked by all, even the unpopular students. She didn't want people to have the impression that she thought she was better than them.

Amy knew a lot of people on campus; although nobody really knew her.

That's okay, she thought, *when the right person comes along who can really be a friend, I'll know it.*

She really did want a close friend. She and her two sisters were so completely different from each other it was hard to imagine that they were even related, let alone friends. Ginny, the baby of the family, was so much younger than Amy … and Cassie … Well, there was just no hope there.

Amy was happy to be out of the house and out from under the thumb and the oppressive reign of her dad and her mother's constant "*tsk … tsk*"ing. This was the sound Mom made whenever Amy and her sisters attempted to do just about anything that Mom disagreed with.

Mom thought Amy should go into nursing because it was a guaranteed job that paid pretty well; thus Amy would never have to be dependent on some man. Mom felt that literature was a waste of time. After all, what could you do with a degree in literature?

"You will never be able to make a decent living … *tsk … tsk.*"

Amy had almost relented, but then realized that she was the one taking out all the loans to go to school.

I should be able to do what I want. So she did. Majoring in literature was no walk in the park. It was only her freshman year and already the reading assignments were overwhelming. But Amy loved to read. Her books were her only true friends. She preferred them to people.

One balmy afternoon, when Amy was walking to the library, she decided to take the long way around campus to get there. The Bradford House, a stately Victorian looking building, was on this route. It looked as though it was undergoing an extensive renovation and restoration. The building normally served as offices for much of the faculty. It was a beautiful edifice, made of granite and marble. It had a long, wide staircase leading to massive, mahogany doors. There were ornate pillars on either side of the front steps. The exterior was nearly covered with thick and thriving ivy, which was carefully trimmed around the tall windows. The restoration was mostly being done on the inside.

As Amy approached the building, she caught sight of a lone figure sitting on one of the steps. He had his back against a pillar. Everything about him was dark. He had long jet-black hair that swept over the collar of his black-leather jacket. He was wearing dark jeans, very old and worn, and scruffy-looking black leather biker boots.

She was momentarily alarmed, but couldn't seem to take her eyes off him.

He very steadily returned her gaze.

Billy was a loner. He had always been a loner. He was smart. He knew that. Maybe too smart for his own damned good. People tended to steer clear of him. It wasn't anything he said. In fact, he rarely spoke, you know, still waters run deep and all that. Billy was an observer. He hovered on the outside, always looking in. What was it then? Billy didn't believe that he was *trying* to look untouchable. He just liked wearing black. He also liked his hair long. Half the time, it hung down over his eyes until he pushed it back by running his fingers through the top of it. This was done in a very James Dean fashion. Billy had great hair, and a lot of it. Was it the silver hoop earring he had pierced through his left nostril? Was it the perpetual cigarette dangling from his lips? Was it the cool, detached gaze he would fix upon someone until they uncomfortably turned away?

He was smarter than most and they didn't even know it. He made As and Bs without even trying. It just came so easily to him. Hell, he had actually received a scholarship to come to this school. An academic scholarship! He had been here for two years and was now something of an icon.

It's respect, he thought. They respected him, they feared him, and they steered clear.

Billy sat on the cool stone steps of the Bradford House. He liked the sounds of the construction going on inside, with the occasional builder walking past him, all dusty, with tools hanging off his belt, saying, "How'ya doin'?" with a nod at Billy.

No judgment. No questions. Just a simple, "How'ya doin'?"

Why can't all people be like that? he thought, as he glanced up at the approaching figure.

Her blonde ponytail bobbed as she walked along. He had seen her before: she was walking into the student bookstore as he was parking his motorcycle, a 1960 Harley he had 'inherited' from his dad. Of course, it wasn't a working machine when his dad had fled the coop, so to Billy the bike was less a well-intentioned gift than something that was abandoned. Billy had worked on the Harley for over a year before he got it running. Supposedly Billy's father had won it in a poker game.

Anyway, the girl hadn't seen him, but he had sure seen her. She was beautiful, in a Sandra Dee kind of way. And here she was again. Was she actually coming over to talk to him? He watched as she approached. She did not turn away, but kept her eyes locked on his.

As she got near, she smiled and lifted her hand in a quick, awkward wave. At this point, she became self-conscious, and looked down at the pavement as she walked on past. He was shocked. This beauty had actually smiled at him! Imagine that! *Beauty and the Beast.*

Amy could feel her heart beating in her ears.

What was that stupid childish wave about? I must have looked like I was in kindergarten or something. He is so cute! A little rough around the edges, but ...

He had not returned her greeting, but he had watched her with eyes that belied his tough exterior. They were large, warm, and brown. Like a puppy-dog. His hair was so shiny the sun reflected off of it like a halo. And here he was trying so hard to look like the devil.

Inexplicably, Amy felt as though she understood him, sort of. He was putting up a wall much in the way that Amy did, though their styles in this effort were entirely opposite. While this fellow seemed to do what he could to ward people off with his almost scary appearance, Amy attracted them, but kept her personal distance by making it all about them. It left her untouched.

Yeah, Amy had seen him around. She had definitely noticed him, but not quite as acutely as she had today.

How do I go about getting to know someone like him? More importantly, would he even want to know someone like me?

Amy was still buzzing with that feeling of anticipation of the unknown when she returned to her dorm room later that evening. She hadn't been able to stop thinking about this guy and the feeling that their lives would definitely cross paths somehow. She could just sense it.

Ada was going through her closet, trying on clothes. Of all things, at 11:00 at night. Her bed was piled with outfits she had discarded after verifying just how flattering they were to her near-perfect figure.

"I'm getting too fat for all my clothes," she wailed as Amy walked in.

"Ada, for crying out loud. There's not an ounce of fat on you."

"Nothing fits!" she said as she examined her lithe body in the full-length mirror she had mounted on the closet door.

"Ada, you look great. Seriously. I don't know what you see, but everyone who looks at you is either jealous or lustful!"

Ada looked at Amy and gave her a doubtful smile.

"Trust me, Ada. You're gorgeous, and in perfect shape. Your clothes fit you like a glove."

Ada stared at her reflection for a minute; then gathered up the clothes on the bed and dumped them on the floor of the closet.

"Well, I'm definitely feeling the need to shop. Wanna go with me to Burlington this weekend?"

Amy didn't have money for things like new clothes, besides, she hated to shop. She was looking forward to doing some reading. She was working through the Jane Austin novels (for the third time), and completely enjoying them, in addition to her assigned reading.

"Umm ... I'm not sure, Ada. I may have to go home to do some laundry ..."

Ada looked at Amy. There was something different about her. She seemed ... *excited* ... about something.

"What's up with you, Amy?"

"Nothing ... nothing. I just know how my Mom is when I—"

"No, not that. I mean, *what's up*?"

Amy looked at her roommate in disbelief.

Good Lord, am I that transparent?

She laughed nervously and averted her eyes.

"Nothing ... nothing," she repeated with a sheepish grin.

"C'mon, Amy. There's *some*thing!"

Wow! Amy thought. She hesitated before venturing into these waters with Ada. She knew Ada loved to gossip. Could she trust her? Amy was just bursting at the seams to tell someone.

"There's this guy—" she stammered.

"I *knew* it!" Ada exclaimed as she pointed her manicured finger at Amy.

"No, it's nothing. I don't even know his name."

"Where'd you meet him?"

"Well, I haven't actually met him ... I've just seen him around."

"What does he look like?"

"Well … he's really cute … in a disheveled kind of way."

"A *disheveled* kind of way?"

"Yeah. He dresses a little rough, kind of like a biker or something. His hair is kinda long, but it's gorgeous. Thick and black … and he's got this earring in his nose—"

"Oh, *God*! You're talking about Billy-the-Bad-Ass, aren't you? Oh God, no, Amy! No, no, no. That guy's trouble with a capital T. You couldn't possibly be interested in him. I've heard that he may have murdered someone … I'm sure he's spent time in jail!"

"Ada, I don't even know him. He just seems so … so … lost."

"Jesus, Amy. Are you sick? The guy's not lost. He's a goddamned predator or something! You need to stay away from him. I can't believe it, of all the guys that are interested in you, and you notice that loser?"

"Ada, it's nothing … and no, I'm *not* interested in him … maybe I just felt … sorry for him—"

"For what?"

"I don't even know." Amy turned toward the bathroom door. "I'm getting ready for bed. I'm really tired."

Amy felt entirely deflated.

Ada fell onto her bed with a humpff. "He's dangerous, Amy. I'm telling you …"

"Don't worry, Ada. It's nothing." Amy disappeared behind the bathroom door.

The weekend arrived.

Ada dragged her on-again, off-again boyfriend, Mac, with her to Burlington. Mac came from money. He would probably pay for Ada's new wardrobe and then she would pay him back in the little motel room he would book for the night. Ada knew how to get what she wanted. The biggest mystery was, did she even know what she wanted?

This was not Amy's problem. In fact, Amy was mad at Ada, anyway. *How could Ada be so judgmental of Billy? At least I know his name now. But Ada had beaten the poor guy up so badly I hadn't even dared ask her what his last name was.*

Amy had already heard some of the crazy rumors about the 'bad-ass', as he was referred to, and that's all they were, rumors. Even though Amy knew that they weren't true; they added to the increasing intrigue she was feeling.

Billy! she thought. Billy was all she could think about, and she wasn't even sure why.

Billy couldn't sleep. He wasn't much of a sleeper, anyway. A good joint would put him in a dreamy state of mind but without the actual sleep. The image of the blonde with the ponytail seemed embedded in his brain. He was trying to picture her naked.

She's well-endowed, he thought lustfully. But it was more than that, and for that reason he was having a hard time picturing her naked. He had never had difficulty with this regarding other girls, or women ...

This girl's different ... something about her...

It was Saturday.

Nothing to do and nowhere to go, thought Billy.

He finished his breakfast of Dr. Pepper and a Twinkie, and then took a long, hot shower, where he took care of business, thinking, not of the blonde with the ponytail, but of the waitress with the deep cleavage who had raised her overly plucked eyebrows and smiled mischievously at him as he wolfed down his burger and fries, and stared her down ... up and down ... feeling like he actually was a wolf!

He frequented the diner fairly often, and it was like a game between Billy and this waitress. He had never acted upon his lust, or her obvious attempts to tempt him. She wore a gold band on her left ring finger, not that it meant much to her. But Billy did use her image in his fantasies. It was very easy to picture *her* naked.

Although this morning in the shower, it was work. The blonde kept bobbing before his eyes. *What the hell IS this?*

A week passed. Billy stayed in the shadows, watching. Observing her became his daily routine. He would stay just out of her sight, leaning against a tree or standing near the corner of a building.

He had discovered her name: Amy.

She *looked* like an Amy. Clean, fresh, full of energy. A good kind of energy.

Other than her various classes, she spent a great deal of time at the library. He noticed that she always took the roundabout route to get there, and always seemed to be searching for something or someone as she passed the Bradford House, peering into the darkened corners behind the entry pillars…

Could she be looking for me? He smiled at the thought.

He wanted to talk to her, but he didn't have a clue as to how to approach her, or for that matter, what on earth he could say. He just wasn't the talkative, sociable type.

Even so, he could sense some kind of connection. A cosmic kind of attraction between them … this girl was effortlessly invading his force-field barriers.

She was being watched. She knew it, and she liked it. She wasn't afraid, as Ada had suggested she should be. She could see Billy out of the corner of her eye. She pretended that she didn't even notice him, which was easy to do with all the mobs of students milling about campus. She kept hoping to see him again on the steps of the Bradford House. Maybe she would actually speak to him. She could sense his interest in her. It didn't feel menacing in any way.

Should I be worried? Maybe Ada's right. Is this guy capable of something really bad, like … rape? Well … Amy thought, *maybe that wouldn't be so bad.*

She turned red at her dirty thoughts.

It was early evening on a Friday. The last rays of the sun reached through the darkened clouds. It created an image that always made her think of God's grace, splayed down upon the undeserving world. It looked as if a storm was on its way. The dark clouds appeared heavy with rain. The sunlight filtering through them had a beautiful, but eerie effect.

As Amy approached the Bradford House, a quick wind whipped up around her, turning the scattering leaves into dancing butterflies. Through the flutter of muted color, she saw him!

He was sitting in the same spot as before, knees slightly apart with his elbows resting on them and his forehead down upon his folded hands.

He looked up suddenly, startled. By her presence? Or just the unexpected blast of wind?

This time he smiled. A brilliant, gorgeous smile. His pleasure in seeing her was blatant. He made no attempt to hide it.

Amy did something she never in a million years thought she was capable of: she walked right up to Billy and sat down next to him.

"Hi Billy."

He was momentarily stunned.

"How do you know my name?" he asked.

"I've done some of my own spying," she teasingly said with a smile. It felt so easy, so natural; she wasn't nervous or self-conscious, or anything!

His face betrayed his embarrassment as it dawned on him that she had been aware of his surveillance.

"Don't worry … I'm flattered … I—"

Billy was overcome and at a loss for what to do or say.

Impulsively, he kissed her on the cheek.

She turned in surprise toward him. They gazed at each other as if they'd known each other forever.

He took her face gently into his hands and kissed her deeply on the lips.

She returned the kiss with everything she had.

That kiss brought them both to an understanding. A bond. A reciprocal yet unspoken commitment. It was destiny. Neither of them felt their usual discomfort when faced with interpersonal relationships. It just felt ... *right.*

Billy looked down at Amy's hands and slipped his into hers.

"I want to show you something," he whispered.

"What?"

"Just come with me."

He pulled her to her feet and led her around to the back of the building. The workers were long gone; all was quiet.

They approached a stand of evergreen shrubs planted against the wall. He parted them with his body and they both entered.

She was not afraid.

There was a small, cool space behind the shrub that hid a below-ground-level window that had plastic loosely taped over it. Billy pulled at the edge of the plastic, which came up easily.

"I'll go first; then I'll help you down."

He climbed into the well, stuck his legs through the window, and scooted his rear toward the opening. The next thing Amy new, he was gone, as she heard the sound of his heavy boots hitting the floor of the room below.

His face appeared at the window. He smiled up at her.

God, he has the most perfect, white smile!

"Come on. I'll help you." His voice was soft and kind of husky.

She climbed in, following his lead by sticking her legs through the opening first. She scooted forward; then felt his hands on her waist. It was a little awkward, but he eased her down to the floor.

The sun's rays were still peeking from behind the clouds, coming in through the front windows in long-cast, magic dust beams.

They were in a ballroom of sorts. The wooden floor stretched across the long, wide, and empty room. Empty, with one exception: a grand piano sat in the corner.

It was absolutely beautiful.

"What is this place?" she asked.

"I don't know. An old dance hall or something. Maybe the faculty has parties down here. It's really cool, isn't it?"

"Wow ... yeah ... " she said in awe.

"Hold on," Billy said as he made his way to the corner behind the piano. He retrieved a brown paper bag.

"What's that?" she asked.

He pulled two pillar-type candles from the bag, and then a lighter out of his jeans' pocket.

"Oh ... so I guess you've been here before?"

"Yeah, I come out here sometimes in the middle of the night when I can't sleep—*by myself*," he added with emphasis.

She watched as he lit the candles. The sharp and pleasant smell of the wicks coming to life added to the magic of the moment.

This was the most romantic thing that had ever happened to Amy in her entire life!

He carefully placed the candles on top of the piano, and then moved around to where the keys were. There was no bench or chair, so he dropped to his knees.

At first, it looked a bit comical. He appeared to be a little boy, too short to reach the keys without piling books on the seat.

But then Billy started to play. It only took a couple of notes for her to recognize *Your Song* by Elton John. His scratchy voice was a little off-key as he quietly sang to her.

Amy was in love already.

In the middle of the song, the sun made its final descent. That's when the rain broke loose. It suddenly pounded fiercely against the windows, drowning out Billy's soft singing, and even the piano.

Billy stopped playing and looked up at her with a silly grin.

She clapped her hands; then started to laugh.

"What?" he said.

"Well ... I guess I just never expected that from you. You are a surprise, Billy. But I have to say ... I had a feeling."

"I had a feeling about you, too."

"Really?"

"Yeah. Really."

They listened to the thundering rain for a minute, looking curiously at each other.

They spent the whole night in that room. No, not what you're thinking. They talked. They talked and talked. Amy poured her heart out about her dysfunctional upbringing and totally insane family. Billy absorbed every word as though it was the most fascinating story he had ever heard.

Then Billy opened up about his own dysfunctional upbringing, which was both shocking and heartbreaking to Amy. And she had thought she had it bad.

She wanted to wrap Billy up in her arms.

He wanted Amy to wrap him up in her arms.

So she did.

He's the one, she thought.

She's the one, he thought.

Present Day

"What's the matter with you? Can't you at least go to the restroom to blow your nose?" Amy hissed at Billy over the nearly empty pizza platter strewn with discarded crusts. "Disgusting pig ..." she muttered under her breath.

Will giggled nervously, and Bobby just stared wide-eyed at Billy, waiting for an explosion.

"Shut up, Will. It's not funny. And finish your pizza, for Christ's sake!" Billy fumed.

Amy looked across the booth at the boys and felt a pang of guilt at their obvious discomfort.

"I'm sorry, Billy," she said with a clenched-tooth smile. "But I would really appreciate it if I didn't have to hear your brains spewing out of your nostrils, especially in a restaurant!"

"First of all, this is not a real restaurant, it's a pizza joint, and—"

"Oh yeah, that's right. I can't remember the last time I saw the inside of a *real* restaurant."

"—and second of all, I can't help it if I have to blow my nose. I'm not doing it to offend you, Amy. It's just a biological necessity sometimes."

"Billy, you can help *where* you do it. Just excuse yourself and go to the bathroom. What are you? A Neanderthal?"

"Jesus, Amy. Give it a rest. I've had a helluva day, and I don't need you on my case. Can't we just eat one meal in peace?"

"You're the one disturbing the peace, Billy. I'm just calling it like I see it, and I'm asking you, nicely, to have some manners. Look at what you're teaching the boys."

Bobby jutted out his little chin. "Can't we just be a *normal* family once in a while?" he demanded.

"Are we not a normal family?" asked Will.

Billy was behind at work. Way behind. His boss had actually called him in to his office the other day. The heat was on. Billy was just so tired these days. He was now taking Ambien regularly and sleeping like a log, but it was never enough. He had a hard time waking up in the morning, and then he'd be running late for work, and be worried about that. He'd take his anti-anxiety meds, but he still felt anxious all day. He was anxious and exhausted.

He started working late in the evenings. *Really* working late.

Come on, Amy, go ahead and call the office to check up on me, he thought. *Not that she ever did. She doesn't give a shit about me. All she cares about is my paycheck.*

He had really been behaving himself lately. He hadn't seen Ginny in a while, longer than usual anyway. The whole thing with Cassie was history.

What had I been thinking?!

He didn't even have time these days to enjoy his favorite 'sport' as he fondly thought of it.

What is wrong with me? I can't seem to think straight. Is it the Ambien?

He couldn't imagine trying to go without what little sleep he got, and he couldn't sleep at all without it.

Oh well ... he'd get caught up. He was working like a damned dog, for crying out loud.

I hate my job. I hate my life. Christ! I'm beginning to sound just like Ginny!

"Wow! You are one handsome fella!" Brenda winked at John as he tried on his old tuxedo. Would it still fit? Yes! She came to him, smoothed the lapels and reached down to button it up for him.

"When's the last time you wore this?"

"Don't ask."

"Oh, come on, when?"

"Aaaaahhh ... I believe it was the last awards banquet at Burlington."

"Oh? The one when you were awarded the Standard of Excellence?"

"Yeah, that would be the one."

"The same night that Vivian told you that she wanted a divorce?"

"The same night. Some timing on her part, eh?"

She regarded him thoughtfully; then began to undo the buttons.

"Time for a new tux, whether this fits you or not." She laughed.

"It is a little outdated, isn't it?"

"No, it looks good on you, no doubt about that. But surely, John, you know I can't marry you wearing a tuxedo with that kind of history in its threads ... you know, we could just go to a Justice of the Peace wearing jeans and sweatshirts. I already feel very married to you. I wouldn't mind."

"Brenda! It's not like we're having a huge wedding or anything, but I want this to be a special day for you—and for me."

"Oh John, you're such a romantic. Okay, we'll dress up, and in a roomful of our friends we will have a wedding—but you will not be in *this* tux!"

"It felt a little loose on me, anyway," he chuckled, and gathered her into his arms.

Brenda rested her head on his chest, and let out a long sigh.

"Sweetie? Are you okay?"

"Oh ...yeah ... it's silly really."

He held her at arm's length, gently questioning, "What's silly?"

"Oh honestly, it's nothing … just some silly phone calls today while you were at work …"

"What phone calls?"

She looked at him and pursed her lips.

"Some girl. She called here three or four times today, asking for John, and then hanging up immediately when I said you weren't here. It was …weird."

"What did the caller ID say?" John's heart began to pound.

"The call was blocked."

He looked down, pensive.

"That is weird," he murmured thoughtfully.

"Do you know who it might have been?" she asked.

"No idea …" he said.

"We're leaving."

"Huh?" mumbled Billy, as Amy pushed at his shoulder.

"We're going, Billy. It's almost noon. You really need to get up. There's ice on the front walkway that needs salting before the mailman or someone else slips and breaks their neck. Do you want to get sued?"

Billy drifted back off to sleep.

"Billy!"

"Huh?"

"What's wrong with you, anyway? Get your fat butt out of bed! What are you going to do? Sleep all day?"

"Leave me alone ..."

"No, Billy. Since you haven't fixed the washing machine yet, I have to take all our dirty laundry to Mom's to get it done. The boys have no clean underwear! So get your ass out of bed and try to accomplish *something* today!" She shoved him hard enough that it actually hurt.

"Damn! Leave me alone ..."

She stared angrily at his disheveled mess of hair, and then stormed out of the room and down the stairs, slamming the door with a bang as she left.

"Great. Now I'll have to fix the door ..." he muttered to himself as he pulled the pillow over his head.

It seemed like only a minute later when the doorbell rang.

She can just use her damned key, he thought, as he held the pillow tight to his ears.

The doorbell rang again, someone's finger insistently planted on the frigging thing.

He peered out from under the pillow until his vision cleared enough to read the bedside clock. *Wow! It was almost 1:30 in the afternoon!*

He dragged himself out of bed, and hollered out as he stumbled down the stairs, pulling a t-shirt over his head. "Just a minute!"

He peeked out the side window to see who it was.

Cassie?! What the hell is she doing here?

He opened the door slowly.

"What do you want?"

"Aren't you going to let me in? It's *freezing* out here!"

He realized then that she was only wearing a tank top and some jeans. *A tank on a tank*, he thought bitterly.

"What are you doing dressed like that in January, for Christ's sake?" he asked.

"Just let me in."

"Amy's not here."

"I know, dummy. She's at Mom's doing her laundry. Let me in, will ya?"

He stepped aside and let her pass.

"What do you want?" he repeated.

"I have something *you* want."

It took him a second to catch what she said; then he shook his head.

"No, no, no … Cassie … that was a mistake. *Really*—"

"Not *that*, Billy. Trust me, I know what a huge mistake that was … Jeez. I'm here to give you … information."

"Information? What information?'

"It's about Amy … she's going to *divorce* you!" she blurted out. "She hates you!"

"How do you know tha—?"

"She really, *really* hates you, Billy!" she interrupted.

"I heard her say that she wishes you were *dead* so she could collect your *life insurance money*."

"What?!"

"I'm telling you, she hates you, Billy. She wishes you were dead." Her voice was now monotone.

"All right … all right, Cassie. Would you just shut up? This is none of your business. I can't believe you came all the way over here to tell me that! Just when did she say this? And who was she talking to, when and *if* she did say it?"

"She *did* say it. I overheard her and Mom talking at Thanksgiving when you and *Ginny* were out walking. She hates you, Billy. You should just leave her." Her eyes started to well up with tears. He could see that she was trembling. At that moment he realized why she was dressed so ridiculously. Cassie was trying in her stupid way to look alluring for him.

Is she nuts? Yeah, she is a total fruitcake! Jesus, what the hell does she want from me?

"Cassie, look, just go home. Amy and I will figure things out."

He suddenly panicked. "You didn't TELL her, did you?"

"No! God, no! I wouldn't want her to know THAT!"

He studied her for a minute. Again, what had he been thinking?

"Okay ... okay ... you need to leave before Amy gets back home. And thanks. Thanks a lot for the ... uhhh ... information." He looked down at the floor, no longer wanting her in his line of vision.

She stood there, unmoving.

"Do you have a coat I can borrow?"

He glanced back at the closet behind him.

"Yeah. Yeah ... go ahead. I think Amy has an old one there in the back that she never wears. She'll never miss it. Just take it and go home, but please don't let her see you in it or she'll wonder why you were here."

He turned away from her and went back upstairs, shutting the bedroom door with the finality of it all.

Cassie dug through the old windbreakers and baseball jackets of the boys' until she came to an over-sized coat way in the back, once purchased by Amy from a thrift store for its vintage look. It was pretty moth-eaten, but looked warm enough. She shrugged it onto her shoulders. It almost fit! Then, she walked out the door.

When Cassie arrived back home, Amy's car was gone. *Good!* she thought, as she pulled into the driveway.

As Cassie walked into the house, Mom looked up from the crossword puzzle she was working on.

"Where'd you get that awful coat?"

"Oh, just some thrift store." She took it off and shoved it to the very back of the coat closet.

~

Cassie threw herself down on the bed, as if the force of her body on the mattress would make a difference somehow.

How dare Billy cast me aside like that!

Her face burned with the thought of showing up scantily clad, very inappropriate for a cold, January afternoon. The message she had attempted to convey was met with a look from Billy of ridicule. What a fool she was. Apparently, Billy thought so too. She was seething with anger. He was the one who started this. Sure, she felt guilty when she considered Amy.

But that's more Billy's responsibility. She is his wife.

The shock on Billy's face upon hearing of Amy's plans to divorce him was evident.

How could he be surprised? Obviously, he's as unhappy in their marriage as Amy. Why else would he seek comfort in my arms?

She remembered every detail of every encounter they had. There really hadn't been that many. Four, in fact, spaced in almost twice as many weeks. It had been like a game between them. Painful for Cassie, but fun nevertheless. Billy had always been so grateful for her willingness to do what Amy wouldn't even have considered. Cassie felt that she had given Billy something almost sacred. The memory of the searing pain brought tears to her eyes now. But it had driven Billy wild.

She, Cassie, had driven Billy wild.

Afterward, but before actually disengaging, he had stroked her back, telling her how special she was to him.

Then all of a sudden, nothing. He had stopped coming over for her, and when he had shown up with Amy, he acted as if they were total strangers!

What an asshole! An appropriate word for a guy who preferred them. *Maybe he's secretly gay?* she wondered. *Maybe that was why he liked that so much?*

It didn't matter anymore. Cassie would *never* let herself be used like that again. She lay face down on her bed and cried.

When her tears dried up, she rolled off the bed, walked downstairs and into the kitchen.

"Hey, Mom, where's that box of pictures? The ones you didn't want to put in the albums?"

"What do you want with those?"

"I just wanted to look at them. I was thinking I might make a collage or something."

"Oh, that would be nice. They're in my bedroom closet, in the back behind my shoes."

Cassie found the box and returned to her room and shut the door. Many of the photos were very old, black and whites from generations past. But there were plenty of Cassie, her sisters, and Billy. This was what she was looking for. She filtered through the box, making a pile of all photos that contained Billy. When she was through, she had a fairly good-sized pile, though most of those pictured Amy as well. Some with the boys.

She got up, went to her bureau, where she had a pack of magic markers and a pair of scissors in her top drawer.

Immediately, she set about meticulously cutting Billy's impression out of each of the pictures. When she was finished, she had a scattering of Billy's cut-away images, strewn over the bedspread. She picked them up, one by one, scrutinizing the practiced smile, almost identical in every snapshot. He obviously favored his left side, because he always seemed to cock his head toward the right, so it was his left side that was actually being photographed. Cassie found this rather amusing, knowing that Billy must be somewhat self-conscious. Lord knows, he didn't act that way at all. He was the most arrogant son-of-a-bitch she knew. But he always got away with it. He was so good-looking.

Cassie went back to the box and started a new search for pictures of herself. She found several, in most she was with her sisters. All of them were pretty good photos. Well, they should be, considering that Cassie had previously gone through them and destroyed any that were unflattering of her. She didn't feel badly about that, even though in so doing, she had destroyed some pretty good shots of her sisters. Ginny had done the same thing with those she had deemed unflattering of her own self.

Cassie went back to the bureau for some scotch tape. She took the pictures of Billy and matched them up to where they covered the image of Amy or Ginny, whoever happened to be in a particular picture with Cassie; then she carefully taped his photo into place.

She had five or six images left of Billy that just wouldn't fit right onto any of the remaining pictures. She studied them for awhile, the edges already starting to curl up without the anchor of their backgrounds. She pulled a black magic marker out of the pack and began to transform each of the unattached images of Billy. She blackened out teeth in some of them, gave Bugs Bunny buck teeth in others, she drew evil eyebrows on some, and totally blackened out the eyes in all of them.

Looking at the mutilated images gave Cassie a sense of satisfaction, but when she looked at the pictures with the transposed, smiling Billy at her side, she felt wistful. If she squinted, it almost looked as if the photo had really been taken that way of her and Billy, a happy-looking couple. She went to her bookshelf and pulled down an old copy of *Alice in Wonderland* and carefully placed the reconstructed photos between the pages.

She returned to the bed, took the vandalized photos, stuffed them into her pocket, and went into the kitchen.

Mom was still working on crossword puzzles. She didn't look up. Cassie went to the junk drawer, where she knew there were several matchbooks. She glanced at her mother as she slid one into her pocket.

Mom took no notice.

Cassie climbed the stairs to the upstairs bathroom, the one she had shared with Ginny and Amy when they were growing up in this house.

She pulled the now crumpled photos out of her pocket, sat on the floor in front of the toilet, and one by one, burned the paper-doll like figures of a grotesque looking Billy. As the paper burned down to her fingers with each photo, she dropped it into the toilet, repeating, "Burn in hell."

The standing rule was that Ginny could only contact Billy through email, and only through the email account he had created specifically for her. Since it had always been Billy's availability that dictated when they would get together, only he could initiate phone contact. Ginny had always obeyed this rule. She did email him frequently, almost daily, in fact. Even if it was only to pass along a silly joke or an article she had found amusing. She often sent him articles about soul mates, true love, and second marriages. It was like she had to remind him daily that she was still there … waiting … waiting … waiting.

Billy actually sometimes got annoyed with her never-ending patience. She had lost his respect long ago—if she had ever had it at all. There had been moments when he had entertained the idea of a future with her. But in reality, it was ludicrous. Billy had never had any intention of leaving Amy, least of all for Ginny. But now Amy was thinking of leaving him?! According to Cassie, anyway. Billy wasn't sure why he couldn't imagine himself leaving Amy. Their relationship was pretty lousy. Nevertheless, he couldn't imagine a life without her. He figured that he could just go on, sticking his fingers into other peoples' pies. People like Ginny. But Ginny seemed to be changing. She had never talked to him the way she did on Thanksgiving. *What was up with that? And who the hell was this John guy?*

What was worse was the fact that she had not sent him one email since. He actually missed what had been so annoying to him before! Something was going on.

Both his wife and his mistress flaking out on him at the same time?

What if Amy knows about Ginny? What if the two of them are in cahoots with each other to somehow destroy me? Ginny is acting so weird, and Amy has never been so distant.

Something was definitely going on, and he needed to find out what.

Billy picked up the phone on his desk and dialed Ginny's number.

"Hi, this is Ginny. You know what to do!" came Ginny's syrupy-sweet recorded greeting.

He hesitated. He did *not* like to leave messages.

Then, in a hushed voice, "Ginny, it's me. Call me. It's important."

He hung up, pissed off that she hadn't been available to take his call. Or maybe she had been there, but had chosen not to answer.

He picked the receiver back up, and dialed the bookstore.

"Read it and Weep. This is Amy, may I help you?"

"It's me."

"Oh! Billy … I'm really busy—"

"How busy can you be at a stupid bookstore? Too busy to talk to your husband? Jeez, Amy, what if I was calling you about an emergency with one of the boys?"

"… Well? Are you?"

"Ummm … no."

"Then what is it?"

"God you make it hard. I was just calling to see if you wanted to go out to eat tonight, like, to a real restaurant or something …"

"A *real* restaurant?"

"Yeah, remember what you said at the pizza place tha—"

"Yeah-yeah-yeah … I remember. But I can't, Billy. Not tonight."

What the hell is this? Amy couldn't possibly have plans. She's always at home when she's not at work.

"What are you talking about, you can't? Jesus, Amy, it's not like I'm calling to ask you out for a date."

"Oh, heaven forbid!"

"You know what I mean. You're my wife, for crying out loud. I'm trying to plan dinner so you don't have to."

"Thanks for sharing the burden of meal preparation, Billy."

"That's not what I meant either. Anyway, what do you mean, you can't?"

"I promised I'd help with the end-of-year inventory tonight."

"What? You never work more than your nine-to-three. Haven't

you always said that? You know, give 'em an inch and they'll take a mile?"

"I know, I know … but I'm making an exception. They really need my help."

"What about the boys?"

"You'll be home by the time I leave to come back here."

"Just how late were you planning on going in?"

"As soon as you get home, I'll leave. I don't know how late I'll be."

Whoa! This is totally not like Amy! She covets her evenings at home with the boys … and she never works extra. She doesn't even like going in for the short hours that she does work!

"What are you gonna do for supper?" he asked.

"I'm just gonna make soup and sandwiches for me and the boys."

"I don't know, Amy … I don't like this …"

"Billy, look, I've gotta go. I'll talk to you later." And with that she hung up.

Billy did *not* like what he was feeling.

~

Brenda was bent over the tub, scrubbing with Ajax and a scouring sponge. The stain on the old claw-foot tub was apparently permanent. She loved this little rental but would be glad when the new house in Stowe was ready. She also loved long baths and was looking forward to soaking in the oversized Jacuzzi tub. She worried though, about the stress of building this new home, plus the demands of a new practice, along with an upcoming wedding, and how it was affecting John. Even *eustress*, 'good stress', was still stress. He seemed so distracted lately.

She thought about the phone calls. It had happened again a couple days ago. Same girl. She had a very recognizable syrupy-sweet voice. Extremely annoying. Brenda had tried to catch her before she hung up. She no longer took the time to tell the woman that John wasn't there, instead she responded with, "Who is this?" or "What do you want?" Of course, the caller hung up without answering her. There was something about this, more than the harassment aspect that was eating away at Brenda. She hadn't mentioned it to John again. She was hoping it would go away, she guessed. But if the girl continued to call, she would do more than tell John. She'd call the police.

She stared at the rust-colored stain that encircled the drain and wearily turned on the water to rinse the clumped Ajax down the drain. She wrung out the scouring sponge and, using the side of the tub, hoisted herself up from her knees. Lord, she was getting old. It felt like she had arthritis or something.

I'm just not going to answer any more of those blocked calls, she thought.

Even better, maybe I can figure out how to block them from coming in! But no, I can't do that without knowing the number from which they originated. What good is technology anyway, if people can foil caller ID?

Oh well, Brenda knew that she was much too curious to find

out who this girl was and what she wanted to block her from calling.

If only she'd call when John was home, then he could answer the phone. The girl must not know John very well if she thought she'd reach him at home during the day. Doctors are never at home during the day. John was hardly ever home period!

She trusted John. She really did.

John decided to try the 'old pal' approach with Ginny. After all, he believed that you caught more flies with honey and surely this buddy-buddy attitude couldn't be misconstrued as anything romantic.

He still wasn't sure where she was coming from. She was totally schizophrenic: coldly polite one minute, girlishly coy the next, and then donning a come-hither look the very next! Very disturbing. Truth be told, Ginny scared the bejeezus out of him. In all of his encounters with crazy nurses, he had never come across one quite so unnerving as Ginny.

He had actually adopted this new attitude with all of the nurses on that unit. He didn't want anybody noticing that he treated Ginny differently than anyone else. Problem was, none of the nurses seemed to be comfortable with him anymore. This whole thing seemed to be escalating and he wasn't even doing anything! He knew it was Ginny who had made the calls to his house. His home! What was wrong with that stupid girl? And what did she want from him? He thought about talking with her nurse manager. He really should try to head it off at the pass but he had no evidence. In fact, the evidence was stacked against him.

If only I hadn't brought in that mistletoe. How can I explain that? What an idiot I am!

~

Ginny was racking her brain, trying to come up with a reason to call John in. She could not understand why he hadn't picked up on her signals. She was going to have to push him. But it was for his *own* good. She could tell this was what he wanted. He was just such a good guy that he was willing to forgo his own desires to keep from hurting that woman … Brenda.

Lord, Brenda sounded so pitifully alarmed when Ginny had called the house.

She sounded scared, for God's sake! What the hell was she scared about? What a ditz! Ginny knew John wasn't there. She was just trying to open the door for that dense man. Brenda *should* be asking John just who this other woman was, and then John could tell her the truth and be done with it! He would be free to pursue the inevitable with Ginny.

Tonight she was going to confront John. She would be supportive, encouraging … but firm. Maybe he was one of those guys that needed to be told what to do. Well, Ginny was capable of doing that. She was sick of waiting. Sick of the games. Lord knows, Billy had been playing with her head for long enough. She wasn't going to take this from anyone else.

She set down the hand mirror and turned to use the toilet. Her stomach was upset.

She still had an hour before she had to leave for work. She was a nervous wreck.

Diarrhea! Great! She could just call in and not deal with it at all tonight … It was the waiting that she couldn't stand. It was literally making her sick. She felt nauseous. *Don't cancer patients smoke pot when they feel this way?*

Whoa. Ginny had never gone to work actually stoned. Hmmm. It would make her feel better … and calmer … she'd probably work better.

She decided to take another quick bath, careful not to get her face wet. Her makeup was halfway done. The warm water was soothing on her inflamed hemorrhoid. One day constipated, the next diarrhea. This was killing her. She decided to take a few drags, just to take the edge off.

She *had* to think of a reason to call John in. Of course, she didn't yet know if she'd even be assigned one of his patients ... it almost felt like she was being monitored at work or something.

The other nurses seemed to be regarding her with some suspicion. She had heard her name and Dr. Gilmore's mentioned in the same hushed whisper ... the sideways glances ... judgmental looks. Were other people becoming aware of their relationship?

~

Ginny felt a little bit numb and a lot paranoid as she walked onto her unit. She busied herself with jotting down her assignment from the board and collecting the charts to check new orders, lab results, etc. She didn't say hello to anyone.

Nobody ever really said much to her anyway, especially lately.

Her co-workers greeted each other and chattered meaninglessly as they prepared their own assignments.

I can't wait for this night to be over, thought Ginny as she entered the break room to get report.

It must be the pot, she thought later, as she made her medication rounds. She couldn't think straight. Everything was in slow motion. She had to put forth extreme effort to focus on giving the right meds to the right patients at the right time.

Shit! I should've just called in. She really didn't feel good.

Two of her patients were Dr. Gilmore's. At this point she didn't even care. She just wanted this shift to be over, and really didn't even want to see him tonight.

She spiked the bag of antibiotic to hang in room 218. She opened the door and realized that the patient was already asleep, but had left the lights on. *Good,* she thought, *I'm in no mood for gabbing with this motor-mouth.*

Mr. Fields, who was in for pneumonia, was moving his lips as if in conversation in his sleep. *Can't even shut up while unconscious!*

Ginny smirked as she hung the medication, unrolled the clamp to allow for a slow drip, and left the room, leaving the light on to make it easier when she came back to switch it over to the maintenance IV fluid.

About an hour later she returned to the room.

Thank God, her buzz was starting to wear off. Now she was just exhausted.

"I don't know if I'm going to make it through this night," she murmured to herself as she made her way to the side of the bed.

Something wasn't right.

Her heartbeat quickened, pulsating in her throat, and her eyes grew wide as she looked down at the figure—a frail, elderly man, lying in the bed.

He was motionless. Absolutely and totally motionless. His skin had a waxy-looking pallor. There was a faint odor of feces.

Ginny stood, staring, unable to move. She began to hyperventilate. She tentatively reached out and shook the patient.

"Mr. Fields?" she rasped through a very dry mouth.

Nothing.

She shook him again, more forcibly.

"Mr. Fields?!"

Nothing.

"Oh shit ..."

Ginny picked up the phone on the bedside table and dialed "0" for the hospital operator.

"Code Blue," she whispered, her throat constricted.

"What? What did you say?" the operator squawked.

"I said ... *Code Blue!*"

The next thing Ginny knew, there was a flurry of activity. The code was being called overhead. The charge nurse, who happened to be Sarah that night, burst through the door.

"Ginny! Jesus! Don't just *stand* there!" as she quickly approached the patient's side, expertly checking his carotid pulse and for any sign of breathing. She pulled the backboard from the end of the bed.

"Help me!" she demanded.

They rolled the patient onto the board. Yes, he had definitely been incontinent of stool.

"You do compressions, I'll do breathing." Sarah bent over Mr. Fields to give the first two rescue breaths.

Ginny numbly went into action. "One and two and three and ..." as she pumped on the man's bony chest.

The code team arrived, bringing equipment, shouting, pushing, and a general chaos. Organized chaos.

All was a whirlwind around Ginny. She felt like she was going to pass out. She moved herself out of the way into a corner of the room.

"Who's taking care of this patient tonight?" came a stern, masculine voice, all too familiar, from the doorway.

Ginny gasped as John Gilmore made his way into the fray.

Amy knew it had been a bad idea. She had been riddled with guilt from the very moment that she told Geoffrey that, yes, she would come by his apartment for coffee later. What was she thinking? She was an old, married woman! Of course, it was all innocent. Just coffee and conversation ... or was it? She had *really* wanted to go to his place; but was scared to death of the idea at the same time. In the very back corner of her mind, she knew it was more than coffee and innocent chatting ... but no, she could not do it. Absolutely not!

Especially now. Of all nights, why did Billy choose tonight to plan a dinner out? It was a sign, she was sure. God was wagging his finger, saying, "No, no, no, Amy..."

Billy *never* called Amy at work. And he *never ever* thought about ways to make Amy's life easier, or more pleasant ... this was just too weird, too coincidental. Yes, it was a sign from God. And it would prevent Amy from doing something bad ... something very bad.

She approached Geoffrey from behind and tapped him on the shoulder. He turned to look at her and smiled his crooked smile.

"Geoffrey ... I can't ... I just can't come over to your place."

The smile disappeared from his face and his brows furrowed.

"Why not?" he whispered. "What's wrong?"

"It's just not a good idea. What if Billy called the bookstore and discovered that I wasn't really here? That it was actually closed?"

"I thought you said that he never ever called you here."

"Well ... he doesn't. But he just did!"

"You're kidding! Why?"

"To ask me to dinner."

"To ask you to dinner? I thought that ... uhh ... Oh! Well ... I understand," he stuttered.

Amy felt a magnetic pull toward this adorable guy. She wanted so badly for him to put his arms around her.

But he didn't.

"I'm so sorry ..." she said.

As Amy turned to go back to the checkout counter, he reached out and grabbed her hand. She stopped and turned back toward him. *PLEASE kiss me*, she thought. *Just go ahead and kiss me!*

"It's okay, Amy. Really, I do understand."

They stood for a moment, holding hands; then Amy awkwardly removed her hand from his and turned away again, stumbling to the counter.

She was angry at Billy. Really angry. He had trapped her in this cursed marriage. She didn't belong with him and her growing feelings for Geoffrey were making that glaringly obvious.

Instead of soup and sandwiches, Amy decided to make dinner for the four of them. Not just any old dinner, but one of Billy's favorites: meatloaf and baked potatoes. Why? She wasn't quite sure. Penance? Maybe.

Dinner was ready at 7:00.

No Billy.

7:15.

Still no Billy.

She called his cell phone.

Voice mail.

She called his office line.

Voice mail.

Annoyed, she hung up without leaving messages.

7:30.

She went ahead and fed the boys, who had been complaining of starvation. She was pretty hungry too, so she sat down and ate with them.

8:00.

Still no Billy.

She was really getting mad. She sent the boys up to get ready for bed; then dialed Billy's cell and office numbers again. Still no answer. She left messages. "Where the hell are you?"

8:15.

The door creaked open and Billy walked in. By this time, Amy was seething with anger.

"Where the *hell* have you been?" she demanded.

"I had to work late. You know I've been behind ..." he said, in an off-hand kind of way.

"Billy! You were *supposed* to come home so I could go in to work. You're just lucky I ended up telling them that I couldn't! What the hell's the matter with you?"

"I kinda think that *my job* is a little more important than your ... *hobby*?"

"You asshole! If you made more money, maybe I wouldn't have to work outside the house as well as inside the house!"

"You hardly work at all."

"WHAT!? I do *everything* around here! I single-handedly take care of the kids, I pay the bills, I clean the house, I do the laundry, I do the shopping, and the cooking. I even made you dinner tonight ... a dinner that went cold while you *thoughtlessly* took your sweet time coming home! The *least* you could've done was to call! You didn't even answer your phones! What the hell were you doing?"

"I told you. I worked late. I didn't answer the phones so I could work without interruption."

"INTERRUPTION!!? You consider your family an *interruption*? You have no idea how lucky you are to even still *have* a family!"

"What the fuck is that supposed to mean?"

"Watch your mouth!"

"*Me* watch *my* mouth? You're the one cussing like a sailor!"

"That's how mad you make me, Billy! Living with you just brings out the worst in me! There is absolutely NOTHING good about this marriage!"

"Maybe if we ever had sex like most married people—"

"SEX!? You must be joking! Maybe if you were more of a MAN—"

"You frigid bitch!" Billy could no longer contain himself. He lunged at Amy and grabbed her left arm, twisting and yanking, his furious red face practically nose-to-nose with Amy. Spittle flew out of his mouth as he spat the words out again. "You are just a frigid bitch!"

Amy swung her free right hand as hard as she could and open-handedly slapped Billy's face.

He was momentarily dazed. He let go of her arm as he reached up to gingerly touch the burning red welt already forming on his cheek.

Amy turned, ran up the stairs, passing by her shocked sons, who stood watching the fiasco on the landing, and locked herself in the bedroom. Her head was spinning. She was panting. She was pacing. She was trembling like a leaf. Her heart was racing.

She could hear Billy on the stairs, murmuring, "It'll be all right," to the boys and telling them to go to bed.

No! It won't be all right! she thought.

"Open the damned door!"

"No!"

"Open the damned door or I'll break it down!" He shook the door handle with enough force to make Amy jump.

The adrenaline was flowing. Amy had never hated anyone as much as she hated Billy at this moment. Her hand stung and her arm was starting to throb with pain. She went to the phone on the bedside table, picked it up, and robotically dialed 911.

"911 Emergency, Washington County. What is your emergency?"

Amy broke into uncontrollable sobs.

"It's my husband … I th-th-think my arm is b-b-broken …"

"Are you in your home?'

"Y-y-yes. I'm in the bedroom … I locked the door … b-b-but he's going to break it down …"

"Stay on the line. We're sending some help."

At that moment, everything went black.

The receiver fell to the floor along with Amy as she passed out.

Billy kicked the door. It only took one swift kick, being so old and loose as it was.

"AMY!" He ran to her side and began to gently shake her. She was already coming to, moaning quietly. Billy noticed the receiver on the floor, picked it up, and placed it back on its cradle.

"What have you done?" Billy harshly whispered.

Heavy footsteps were heard coming up the stairs, mingling with the patter of little bare feet.

"Police. What's going on here?" asked a manly man's voice just beyond the doorway.

Amy fuzzily pulled herself up so she was leaning on both elbows, wincing as she put weight on her left arm.

Will appeared at the door with two uniformed cops dwarfing him from behind.

With Billy's very gentle assistance, Amy got up to a standing position.

"Oh, officers, I'm fine … everything's fine. Will, honey, go to bed," Amy said in the most normal voice she could muster.

"Just a little spat," said Billy. "We're fine, aren't we, honey? But thanks guys, thanks for coming …" as if *he* had been the one to call for help.

"With all due respect, sir, we need to hear the story from your wife. Again, ma'am, what's going on?"

"We just had an argument. It's fine now … really … I wasn't thinking straight when I called," she responded.

"How about your arm, ma'am? What can you tell us about that?"

"It's fine too," she answered.

"Well … let's take a look."

"We're letting you go, Ginny. You're fired."

They had subjected her to drug testing after the 'incident'. It was protocol following an error of that magnitude. It had come back positive, of course.

"I swear I've never done that before … and I'll never do it again. I was sick … nauseous … you know, like a cancer patient? I thought it would help. I promise! I'll never-ever—"

"Please, Ginny. You are very fortunate at this point that there is no one to press charges against you. Clean out your locker and leave. And you should know that you'll have to appear before the Board. You will most likely lose your license."

"My license? What do you mean? How will I get a job?" Ginny's voice was shaking and cracking as she did her best to remain composed.

"I don't believe that you realize the gravity of what you've done, Ginny."

"I do … I do! I can't even begin to say how sorry I am."

"Sorry won't bring Mr. Fields back, Ginny."

"Don't I have the option to go to counseling, or rehab or something?"

"The Board will present your options at your meeting with them."

"Will I still lose my job if I do what they say?"

"Ginny, you've already lost your job. This incident was preceded by several complaints."

"Complaints? From who?"

"Whom," she corrected. "You would have heard about them in your next evaluation, which was scheduled for next week. At this point, it no longer matters."

"It *does* matter. I need to know who complained, and about what!"

"Ginny, this meeting is over. Like I said, please clean out your locker and leave now. And by the way, if I were you, I would *not* compare myself to a cancer patient … *honestly*!"

With that, her manager turned her back on Ginny to put the file into the cabinet behind her. When she turned around she gave Ginny a cold glare.

Ginny stood up. Her legs felt like Jell-O. She turned and fumbled with the doorknob as her once-friendly nurse manager watched her leave.

~

"She killed a patient!"

"What!?"

John shook his head as Brenda looked at him in utter disbelief.

"She gave the wrong antibiotic to a patient with severe allergies. She was high on pot at the time."

"You're kidding ... and *she's* the one who's been calling for you?"

"I'm pretty sure of it. She's a total nutcase. I tried really hard to be nice to her, but I guess it backfired ..."

"I'll say. Is she a danger to us?"

"I don't think so."

"We should take out a restraining order."

"Oh Brenda ... I don't think that's necessary."

"Well I do!" Brenda turned and abruptly started folding the clothes from the basket she had brought in earlier.

John reached down to help her by grabbing a bath towel and whipping it out sharply before beginning to fold it neatly.

They worked together silently for a few minutes, piling jeans, sweaters, and scrubs onto the bed.

"All right Brenda, if it will make you feel better."

"Well it should make *you* feel better, John. She's obviously unstable."

"Yes ... you're right. I'll do it first thing Monday morning."

"What about the patient's family?"

"He didn't list any next of kin or even any person to contact on his admitting forms. It looks like he was all alone in the world."

All Brenda could say was, "That is so sad."

"Yes, it is sad; but fortunate for the hospital ... and for Ginny. There's nobody to file a lawsuit."

"Oh John ..."

Later, as John showered for a dinner party being thrown in his and Brenda's honor, he heaved a great sigh of relief. This lunatic girl would finally be out of his life. He was so elated at the turn of events that he had to remind himself that it had been at the cost of a patient's life. The man had been eighty-six years old, he thought. And nobody had ever come to visit him in the hospital, he reasoned. Just a lonely, very old man ... Damn! How could he be thinking this way? That Ginny sure showed her true colors. Now everyone could see clearly that it had all just been her weirdness.

Hmm ... eighty-six years old. The man had lived a very long life.

John wondered if any family might come out of the woodwork. Well, the chart was very clearly marked, with his own handwritten admitting note citing the poor man's severe allergy to Penicillin. That idiot nurse! She deserved a lot more than just losing her job. When he had met with the nurse manager, he had verbalized that he'd been having reservations regarding Ginny's stability. He told her that Ginny's behavior had been inappropriate more than once, but being the kind man that he was, he had felt it important to give her the benefit of the doubt. How he wished he had said something sooner! He also informed the manager of his suspicions regarding the phone calls made to his home. She told John that some of Ginny's coworkers had also noticed Ginny's odd behavior, especially where he was concerned. He was now sure that in the nurse manager's mind, Ginny was the problem. And of course she was! And now she was GONE!

Poor, old Mr. Fields.

~

Amy stumbled aimlessly through the house. It was 4 a.m. and Billy was in the slammer. He was going to be so *mad* when he got home, which would be later today. One of the officers, who happened to also be a paramedic, had examined her arm. He said it wasn't broken but he advised her to keep it elevated and on ice, then follow up with her doctor if it was not better in a day or two. She had swallowed a couple of Billy's Vicodin, which he kept in good supply due to his frequent "migraines". Amy didn't like the fact that Billy kept such an arsenal of drugs, and wasn't quite sure how he was able to procure so many, but at the moment she was grateful. She felt no pain. The boys were finally asleep. It took her over an hour to finally convince them that Billy would be back at home today. She had not pressed charges and had begged the officers not to take Billy to jail. They had told her that they had no choice. In a domestic altercation they had to take the offending party to "cool off" for a twelve-hour stay. They assured her that he would have no record, and that this was for the safety of both of them. They obviously didn't know Billy! He was going to be absolutely steaming mad when he got home!

Maybe she should just leave? Maybe this was the push she needed to move on with her life … cut her losses … start fresh?

She felt badly for having called the damned police in the first place. What had she been thinking? Well, that was the problem … she hadn't been thinking. It had been like she was on autopilot or something. He *had* hurt her … although that was so out of character for Billy. He must be really upset about something. He had never laid a hand on her in all their years of marriage. And they had had some pretty bad fights. Could he have a clue about her growing feelings for Geoffrey? Geoffrey … it was utterly ridiculous for her to even think this way, let alone feel this way … but was Geoffrey her soul mate? The one she was supposed to be with? How stupid for her to even be considering this. She was so much older and with two children, for God's sake!

But maybe she should leave—just for a while … like a separation or something. She certainly had enough money to get an apartment for a few months. The boys could stay right here in their home. She could still pick them up from school every day, bring them home, feed them dinner, and then go to her apartment when Billy got home … and on weekends the boys could stay with her! It might be like an adventure for them!

At this point Amy stopped pacing and flopped down on the couch. Her tears were bitter, the pain in her heart almost tangible, despite the numbness in the rest of her body.

It was time to go. Time to make a change. She and Billy would have a long, heart-to-heart after he got home.

Ginny was in shock. Desperate times called for desperate measures. She called Billy's cell phone, a no-no. It rang several times before it was finally answered.

"Hello?"

"Oh! Uhh ... Amy? Why are you answering Billy's phone?"

"Ginny! Oh God! Ginny! Billy's in jail! And it's my entire fault!"

"In *jail*? What are you talking about?"

"Oh my God, Ginny ... I don't know what to do! I *told* them it was my fault, but they took him away anyway ..."

"All right, all right ... take a deep breath. Start at the beginning. What *happened*, Amy?"

Ginny's wheels were turning. Had Billy told Amy about Ginny? No, of course not ... Amy probably wouldn't be talking to Ginny right at this moment if he had. It hadn't even seemed to register to Amy that Ginny had actually called Billy's number! She was extremely distraught.

Ginny waited patiently through all of Amy's "Oh my Gods" until she was able to start telling the story.

Of course, Amy didn't tell Ginny the *whole* story, just that they had had a huge fight and it had gotten a little out of hand ...

"Amy, I can't believe you called the police on Billy."

"I know, I know, I know!"

"How is your arm?"

"Oh, it's fine. I took some of Billy's pain meds ... Hey, Ginny! *You* could pick Billy up for me, couldn't you? They said he'd be out sometime today. I'm not sure when, but you could call the station and find out."

"Jeez Amy! Shouldn't *you* be the one to get him?"

"Ginny ... he's going to be furious with me. Maybe you could defuse him before he gets home."

Ginny was silent for a few minutes while she contemplated the scenario. She really needed Billy about now, but what frame of mind would he be in after *this*? Well, maybe she was just what Billy needed about now, too.

Maybe they could talk seriously about their future together, especially now that that asshole John Gilmore was no longer an option. What a frigging jerk! Ginny probably wouldn't have been fired if it hadn't been for that pansy-ass tease. She was sure that any complaints about her had come from him.

"Okay, I'll do it."

"Oh Ginny, *thank* you!"

"Maybe I'll take him somewhere to talk for awhile before I bring him home ..."

"That would be great. Just try to calm him down. Make him understand that I was in so much pain, I wasn't thinking straight when I called 911."

"I'll do my best, Amy."

Billy was mad alright. Fuming, furious, outraged, peeved, angry … there were not enough words to describe his wrath.

"What the hell are *you* doing here?"

"Is this the thanks I get for coming to pick you up?"

Billy walked past Ginny and stormed through the door of the police station.

Ginny followed him out and glared at the officer behind the desk as she did so.

"Where's your car?"

"Just down the street … *Billy*!"

"*Thank you*. Okay?"

"Damn it, Billy. I don't even know why I came."

She turned and headed down the street toward her car. This time it was Billy's turn to follow.

She got into the car and reached over to unlock the passenger door for him.

He heaved himself in and slammed the door.

They both stared out the front windshield in silence.

Finally,

"I'm sorry, Ginny. Thanks for picking me up. How did you even know I was here?"

"Amy told me."

"What the hell? Did she notify the newspapers too?"

"No, Billy. Calm down. She didn't call me, I called her."

"Oh … well, why didn't *she* come to pick me up?"

"She thought you'd need time to calm down."

"Well that's an understatement!"

"Let's go to my place."

"Are you nuts?! In case you can't tell, things have never been worse between me and Amy. Are you trying to push it over the edge, Ginny?"

"Your marital problems *are not my fault*. I'm trying to help you here. Amy actually asked me to. She's not even expecting you home for awhile … so what do you want to do? I can just drop your ass off at home if that's what you want."

Billy fumed for a few minutes as he took all this in.

Ginny held her breath, and patiently waited for his answer.

"Fine. Let's go to your place … but wait, I must've left my cell phone in the station …"

"No, you left it at home. Amy actually answered it when I called."

"You called my fucking cell phone?"

"Don't worry, Billy. She took it completely in stride. I don't know why you ever worried about that anyway. She knows, or thinks, that you're like a brother to me."

"You stupid bitch. I told you not to call my cell. Ever."

"Damn you, Billy. All you ever think about is yourself! I was having my own personal crisis! I lost my *job* yesterday!"

Billy looked at her blankly, until what she said finally registered. She looked right back at him as she waited for his reaction.

After a minute or two, they both started to laugh.

"Aren't we a pair? Me, a jailbird. You, an unemployed bum."

"Yeah …"

They both resumed their somber faces and dour moods.

"So, what are you gonna do?" he asked.

"I have no idea. What are *you* gonna do?"

"I'm gonna go home and fuckin' kill Amy."

"Don't say stupid things like that, Billy."

"I swear, I don't know what that bitch is trying to do to me. She's got something up her sleeve."

"You could just move in with me. Wasn't that the original plan anyway?"

"Ginny, I can't just move in with you. How would that look?"

"Who cares how it looks? For Christ's sake, Billy, it would look the way it is, and has been … forever!"

Billy looked at Ginny without responding. She looked like shit, despite the obvious time she must have spent applying the tons of makeup she wore. Her lips were dry and there were flakes of lipstick on her teeth. She hadn't touched up her roots and Billy could see that she was starting to sprout some grays. She was skinnier than she usually was...in a sickly kind of way.

"What the hell's wrong with you, anyway? Why on earth would you wait all these years for something that obviously is not going to happen?" he asked snidely, with contempt in his voice.

She turned toward the window and started to cry.

He couldn't bring himself to comfort her.

"Don't you have a new boyfriend anyway? John, *the doctor*?"

Ginny started to cry even harder. She turned toward Billy, mascara smeared down her face, her nose running.

"He's part of the reason I got fired."

"How's that? What happened?"

Ginny told Billy about how John had flirted mercilessly with her, kissing her in the stairwell, making innuendos and suggesting that they had a future ... but apparently after what happened with his patient, he had changed his tune. She then went on to describe what happened in the hospital that night. She was sure that John was distancing himself so that no blame could end up on him, and to make certain of it, he had even said things to her nurse manager to make Ginny look bad. He was nothing but a scumbag.

"Damn, Ginny. You sure know how to pick 'em."

"Yeah, well, I picked *you*, didn't I?"

"Ginny ... "

She wiped her nose on her sleeve, then swiped with both hands under her eyes to wipe away the tears and mascara. She stared out the windshield.

Her mood was quickly changing from self-pity to anger. Billy could sense it.

"I just need to figure things out, Ginny. Please take me on home. We'll talk later. I can't think straight right now."

"Fine."

She started the engine and peeled away from the curb. Within minutes, she screeched to a halt in front of Billy's house, and he quickly opened the door and jumped out, grateful to be alive after the reckless drive from the jail.

"Thanks a lot," he said as he slammed the door shut.

After Billy got out, the car felt incredibly empty, like a big, dark cave, hollow and echoing. His horrible words were what bounced around in the emptiness. "Why would you wait around all these years for something that obviously is not going to happen … not going to happen … not going to happen …" He had never said this to her before, just like he had never said, "I love you."

But just as Ginny knew way down deep that he truly didn't love her, she was also knew the truth of his words today. If he had even an ounce of kindness in him, he would have made that clear from the beginning instead of leading her on and wasting her life. She was an idiot; a pitiful excuse of a human being. She had *nothing* in her life, and her future was certainly looking less than bleak. She had lost her job. Possibly her license! Why on earth would she have had the lousy luck to have been assigned one patient on antibiotics with a severe allergy to Penicillin, and another patient who just happened to be on Penicillin? Because this was her luck, her *bad* luck. It was the story of her life.

She wanted to feel badly about the patient, Mr. Fields, but was incapable of feeling anything but sorry for herself. She was actually pissed that the man had been assigned to her in the first place. She put the car in drive and burned rubber as she tore away from the curb. She drove fast and recklessly as she made her way back to her apartment, her hot tears blurring the road in front of her. She ran a yellow light, and —

BAM!

Her car broadsided a garbage truck crossing the intersection.

Her face came down hard, her nose cracked as it hit the steering wheel, and then her head snapped back, fortunately hitting the headrest.

The driver of the garbage truck was at her window in seconds.

"Christ, lady! Are you all right?!" He rapped his thick, filthy knuckles on the glass.

She shakily rolled down the window, blood pouring out of her nose as she tried to catch it in her cupped right hand.

She could already hear the sirens working their way toward them.

"Are you all right?!" he repeated.

"I doht doh … I doht doh …" Sounding like someone with a very bad head cold.

"Help is on the way … *Christ*, lady!"

Ginny allowed herself to be transported by ambulance to Mercy's ER, where she was examined and then sent home with a splinted and bandaged broken nose. She had been flagged in the system as a potential substance abuser; thus had been advised to use extra-strength Tylenol for the pain. Her nose ached as though someone had taken a hatchet to it. She couldn't wait to get home to the little stash of Vicodin she had earned while in servitude to Billy. Fuck the hospital!

Her car had been taken to the police station so she needed a ride. She certainly couldn't call Billy or Amy right now, and she sure didn't want Mom to know any of this just yet, if ever.

She called Cassie.

Cassie was excited to come to the rescue of one of her 'perfect' sisters. She was a nonstop chatterbox on the drive to Ginny's apartment. She would make some chicken noodle soup! They could watch a movie together Cassie would stay for as long as Ginny needed her! It was so nice to be needed!

Ginny didn't have the heart or the energy to put up a fight. Besides, she would need Cassie later when she went to pick up her car …

Putting up with Cassie was not nearly as intolerable as Ginny had anticipated. Cassie seemed to be quite eager to play the caregiver role.

Ginny took three Vicodin and had a devil-may-care attitude. She ate the soup Cassie heated up for her, and then the two of them lounged around in the living room, watching movie after movie on HBO. They ordered a pizza and stayed up late watching more TV.

When Ginny started to nod off, Cassie tucked her into bed and went to sleep on the couch.

Ginny woke up the next morning to the aching pain of her nose. She stumbled to the bathroom and took three more Vicodin. She glanced into the living room and looked with a mixture of pity and embarrassment at Cassie's large form spilling over the edges of the couch and out from the corners of the blanket. At the same time, she felt a surge of love for her older sister. She had really been sweet last night! Maybe she and Cassie could get a two-bedroom apartment together. Ginny would surely get a job doing something but if she couldn't work as a nurse, she just didn't see how she was going to make ends meet on her own. Cassie couldn't be making much money flipping burgers part-time. Ginny did *not* want to have to do that kind of work. But of course, *she* wasn't Cassie.

She went back to bed wondering if maybe Cassie had amassed a small fortune working her menial job while living with Mom and having absolutely no household expenses, and to consider the possibilities until she drifted back to sleep.

Cassie woke up in a foul mood. She hadn't slept a wink on that uncomfortable couch. And Ginny hadn't thanked her once for all she had done for her! What? Did Ginny think Cassie owed her something?

Cassie went into the kitchen and started banging around, opening and shutting cupboard doors and drawers without any regard to the sleeping Ginny. She finally found the coffee and filters; then had to figure out how to work the new-fangled fancy coffee maker that Ginny owned.

She looked around the apartment. Ginny had really nice stuff! It pissed Cassie off.

I should have an apartment this nice. Even Mom doesn't have things as expensive as what Ginny has. But Mom's house is much cleaner, much neater, and more comfortable … homier. Ginny's problem is she has too much stuff!

~

When Billy got home, Amy was asleep on the couch. The boys were upstairs playing video games in their room. His first instinct was to wake Amy up and demand an explanation for her stupidity last night; make her aware of what a hellish night he had spent in the slammer because of her. But, as he looked at her arm wrapped in an old Ace bandage and sling left over from one of the boys' mishaps, he felt a pang of guilt for his own behavior, and an overwhelming sudden affection for this woman who, apparently, was beginning to hate him.

He decided to take a shower. He knew that he looked and smelled like crap. He sure felt like crap.

After looking in on the boys, who glanced up at him with a preoccupied "Oh, hi Dad." he made his way into the bathroom. He closed the door and stood looking at the two ratty bathrobes hanging on pegs on the back of the door, one pink, one green.

It began as a quiver, a quick catch of his breath, and then the sobs overtook him. He sat down on the toilet seat, shaking uncontrollably; tears and snot running down his face as he pulled at his hair.

He wasn't sure how long he sat there in that state, but eventually his breathing evened out, the tears dried up, and he heaved himself up off the toilet seat to turn on the shower.

Amy woke up to the sound of the shower running. She was still pretty groggy from the pills she had taken. Her body was not used to that stuff. The water ran for what seemed a very long time before she finally worked her way upstairs to knock on the bathroom door.

"Billy?"

No answer.

She knocked again, louder.

"Billy?"

"I'll be out in a minute," came his monotone reply.

She stopped at the boys' room before heading back downstairs.

"Hey guys!" she said, trying to sound upbeat. "Dad's home … just like I told you he'd be!"

"Yeah, we know."

"We saw him."

Then, in unison, "What's for lunch?"

They had not taken their eyes off the television screen or their hands off the video game controllers.

Amy was tired. Just plain tired.

"I'll make some grilled cheese sandwiches and tomato soup. Come on downstairs," she said, and then turned to head down to the kitchen to her never-ending motherly chores.

Not knowing Billy's state of mind, Amy decided to wait until tomorrow to tell him of her plans. They had been through enough over the past twenty-four hours.

The smell of food—melting butter, cheese, and warm soup—brought them tumbling down the stairs. Billy's bare feet plodded down shortly afterward. Amy had somehow managed to cook this simple meal one-handedly, and was awkwardly filling bowls and putting the sandwiches on plates, as Billy sat down in his place at the head of the table. He was wearing his bathrobe and seemed to be examining the collar as he pulled at a loose thread.

"How long have we had these bathrobes?" he asked Amy.

"Uh … I don't know. A long time," she replied, looking at him in puzzlement.

"They're so old."

"Yeah, they're old, Billy. What? Do you want me to go out and buy you a new one?" she asked impatiently.

He looked up at her. His eyes were red and puffy.

"No … they're just old enough to be comfortable. I don't want a new one."

And that was all they had the energy to say to each other on that exhausting afternoon.

Cassie's jealousy felt raw, and was momentarily overpowering. What was she even doing here? Ginny never did *anything* for Cassie. Most of the time, she wasn't even *nice* to her.

Ginny's cell phone was sitting on the kitchen table, and startled Cassie as it blared out, "Dadadada-dada-dada ..." in the tune of *Super Freak*. Impulsively, she reached down, picked it up, and looked at the caller ID.

Billy? What on earth would he be calling Ginny for?

Cassie really didn't want to have to speak to him, but her curiosity and suspicion made her answer the phone.

"Hello?"

"Look, Ginny, I really am sorry about what I said to you," Billy whispered in a rush. "I honestly don't know what the future holds, but I do know that I don't want you out of my life. You've gotta know that I just wasn't acting like myself. It'd been a pretty damned stressful night."

Cassie remained silent as she processed what she was hearing Billy say, in utter disbelief.

"Ginny? You're still my girlfriend, aren't you?"

Cassie quickly hung up the phone without responding. Then she turned the phone off. She was literally quaking with anger.

What the hell was going on here? Did Ginny and Billy have a RELATIONSHIP!? Who the hell did he think he was? And who the hell did Ginny think SHE was?

The blood was pounding in Cassie's ears.

She ran to Ginny's cupboards and started pulling dishes and glasses out of them, hurling them at the walls. The sound of crashing glass and pottery were enough to wake the dead.

Which it did.

Ginny appeared in the doorway, eyes wide, hair disheveled, mouth wide open in horror as she dodged a heavy plate thrown right at her.

"*Cassie*, what the fuck are you *doing*?" She dodged a wine glass that whizzed by her head, grazing her hair before it smashed into the wall.

She came to her senses and ran into the bathroom, locking the door behind her.

Cassie came running after her, screaming at the top of her lungs, “I’ll kill you, you bitch!” She pounded on the door and violently shook the handle.

From the other side of the door, Ginny was truly fearful for her life. Cassie had always been off balance, and now something had pushed her over the edge.

“Cassie! Cassie! Calm down, please! Talk to me! For God’s sake, Cassie, *what* is wrong? Please stop, Cassie—”

“You *know* what’s wrong. You know exactly what’s wrong … or should I just ask BILLY?!”

Ginny’s mind was racing. Had she left her secret email account open on her laptop? Had she left out any of the polaroids she and Billy had taken of themselves in compromising positions? No, surely not. She kept those safely hidden in a hole she had cut out of *War and Peace.* Besides, Billy never let his face be photographed. It could be anyone’s penis or ass in those pictures … What could Cassie possibly know? Had Ginny talked in her sleep? Mumbled something during last night’s stupor?

“Cassie, what on earth are you talking about?”

“You *know*, you husband-stealing bitch!”

“No, Cassie! I have no idea what you’re talking about. Honest!”

Cassie stopped pounding and kicking at the door. Ginny heard the sound of her overweight burden of a body heave itself to the floor. She was sobbing.

“Billy just tried to call you …” she managed through her angry tears.

“Billy? Called *me*? Why would Billy be calling me?”

“He wanted to know if you would still be his GIRLFRIEND!”

Ginny was flabbergasted.

“What? Cassie, what exactly did he say to you?”

“When I answered the phone, he thought I was YOU!” Cassie spat out.

Oh, Jesus. Holy crap! thought Ginny. *What the hell did Billy say? This is great… just great.*

"Cassie … whatever Billy said … he was just joking around. He jokes around like that sometimes."

Cassie was silent for a minute.

"So he just calls you sometimes like that, out of the blue? Then he jokes around about you being his *girlfriend*? And you expect me to believe that?" Cassie asked sarcastically.

"Yeah, Cassie … he does. But you have to understand … he's kinda making fun of me … because I don't *have* a boyfriend … besides, he doesn't call that often … hardly ever."

"Then why did you act so shocked at first when I said he called?"

"Like I said, it doesn't happen all that often. I don't even remember the last time I talked to him!"

Cassie didn't respond, but tucked this little lie behind her ear. She *knew* by what Billy had said that they had recently been talking to each other.

"Honestly, Cassie, I have no control over what Billy says or does." She felt as though she were treading water—in an ocean full of rogue waves and lurking sharks.

Cassie still did not respond.

"Listen, Cassie, I don't know what Billy's up to, and frankly, I don't care. But I have been thinking about something that might interest you … I was actually wondering if it might be fun for you and me to get an apartment together!"

Oh crap, crap, crap… She didn't mean to say that. Living with Cassie was out of the question. This outburst was proof of what a very bad idea this was. But, maybe just the idea of it would calm Cassie down and make her forget about Billy's call.

"… Really?"

"Yeah, Cassie … Can I safely come out now?"

Cassie giggled; then in a high-pitched squeal she said, "That would be waaay cool!"

Ginny slowly unlocked the door, opened it a crack, and peered out. Cassie sat like a mound of lard on the floor of the narrow hallway. She looked up at Ginny with eyes that were bright and a bit on the maniacal side. She reminded Ginny of Charles Manson.

Cassie sucked in a deep breath of air and started babbling.

"We could really fix it up nice ... an apartment! You've already got *really* nice stuff! I'll bet Mom would give me some furniture and other things we might need! I've got some money saved up. I could buy curtains, or towels ... or new DISHES..." she said with another inappropriate giggle, as she surveyed the broken glass on the hallway floor. She went on,

"We could stay up late every night and order pizza. We could go shopping together or to movies. This is a GREAT idea, Ginny!"

"Yeah ... yeah..." Ginny was already trying to backpedal. "But we'd need a two-bedroom, two-bath, of course. Do you think you make enough money to pay your half of the bills, Cassie?"

"I'm sure I do! And if I have to, I'll get more hours at work!"

Wow! It was totally frightening how Cassie's personality could switch, *presto-chango*, so dramatically. Ginny wasn't about to piss her off again.

"Well, okay then. Let's start thinking about it and maybe start looking around for just the right place ..."

"That shouldn't take long—there are LOTS of apartments!"

"Yeah, but a lot of them we won't be able to afford, and a lot of the ones we could afford are pretty gross ... it may take some time to find the right one for us."

Ginny noticed a dark cloud passing over Cassie's eyes.

"... but I'll start looking right away!" she finished.

After putting the boys to bed on Sunday evening, Amy decided to broach the idea of a separation with Billy. He was sprawled on the couch, watching television. They had hardly spoken ten words to each other since he had come home yesterday afternoon. When she walked into the living room, she realized he was actually asleep. Exasperated, she picked up the remote, punching the Off button.

"Hey … what are you doing?" asked Billy groggily.

"Billy, you fell asleep watching TV."

"I wasn't asleep. I just had my eyes closed for a minute …" he said as his eyes went half-mast again.

"Billy, we need to talk."

"About what?" he asked as his eyes closed.

"I think we should do some kind of trial separation."

Billy's eyes opened and he wearily pulled himself into a sitting position.

"Amy… for crying out loud. We had a *fight* … that's what married couples do."

"No, they don't Billy. At least not like us. All we *do* is fight. I can't take it anymore. I'm moving out for awhile. The boys can stay right here with you while we figure things out. I'll pick them up from school every day and feed them dinner here. Then, when you get home, I'll leave and go to my place, wherever that is."

"You're *not* going anywhere, Amy."

"Just watch me, Billy." And with that she turned and went upstairs.

Billy wasn't sure what to think or feel. She had sprung this on him while he was practically asleep. He had already taken his Ambien and was having a hard time even processing the conversation.

Where the heck could Amy go? If she went to her Mom's, which was the only place she could go, it surely wouldn't be long until she was begging to come back home.

He drifted back off to sleep on the couch.

~

The next morning, Billy woke to the sounds of Amy and the boys getting ready to leave for the day.

"Why didn't you wake me up? I'm going to be late for work," he demanded.

"Billy, you're a big boy. You're gonna have to learn how to take care of yourself."

Their vague conversation of last night came flooding back to him.

"You are not leaving, Amy."

"Yes, I am. In fact, I'll probably be out of here by tonight. I'll talk to the boys about it on the way to school. We gotta go … Come on, boys," she yelled.

The boys came clattering down the stairs.

"Get your coats."

There was a flurry of activity as coats were put on, book bags and lunches grabbed, and then they were gone.

"Bye, Dad!" echoed in the suddenly silent house.

Billy contemplated calling in sick. He was already in the hot seat with his boss for falling behind on claims, even though he was working as hard and fast as he could. As much as he despised his job at the moment, he didn't want to get canned. He should probably just go in.

Hell, if Amy needs some time away, then FINE, she can just move her ass right on out.

He looked around at their modest home. Even though they were just renting, Amy had put a lot of blood, sweat, and tears into this place. She had painted every wall herself, mostly warm earth tones. Each wall had something hanging on it, be it a tasteful print, a carefully arranged group of framed family photos, or a dried wreath that Amy had made herself.

This looks like the home of a happy family. What the hell does she have to be so unhappy about?

He provided a pretty decent life, dammit!

He went into the kitchen to get himself a cup of coffee. There sat the coffeepot. Empty. Amy preferred hot tea in the morning, but still always made a pot of coffee every day.

"You're a big boy now. You're gonna have to learn to take care of yourself." He mimicked her in a whiny voice in the empty room.

If anyone should be unhappy in this relationship, it's me. I sure don't ask for much. She works her little part-time job doing what she loves to do anyway, surrounded by books ... she has a nice home to live in ... I am pretty damned easy-going ... but all she ever does is complain! Nothing is ever good enough for that bitch.

He should have known from the start that she'd become all high and mighty. For crying out loud, she treated him like a kid instead of a man, always correcting him, telling him how to drive, what to do—totally emasculating him!

I'll show her! I can take care of myself just fine without you, Amy, thank you very much.

He set about making coffee, which turned out weak and watery. He looked up at the clock. *Shit! Late again!*

He'd grab a Starbucks on his way in.

Amy sat in her car up the street from the house until she saw Billy leave.

She was filled with a mixture of emotions as she walked into her home. She had taken this house and single-handedly made it into a home. She had done it for the boys… and for Billy. He didn't even care. He just took it all for granted. It was like he was old-fashioned in the sense that he assumed that she'd take on all the "woman's work." He just expected it and never showed appreciation of any kind. If she was supposed to do all the "woman stuff," shouldn't it follow that he do all the "man stuff?" Well, first of all, he didn't make enough money. On top of everything else, she still had to go out in the workforce. She had to bring home the bacon, fry it up in a pan … and did he think that she was supposed to never let him forget he's a man?

Like hell!

She had to remind him constantly of the little things, like taking out the trash. He never even noticed when something needed to be fixed, and then would require being asked three or four times at *least* before getting around to it, at which point, Amy would be beyond mad.

Amy hadn't researched what the apartment scene was like yet. She did know that most were unfurnished. Would it cost a lot more to rent a furnished one? Did she even want to sleep on a bed or sit on a couch that someone else had been lounging all over, and God knows what else? Someone she didn't even know? Possibly someone gross?

Maybe she should stay with Mom or Ginny for a few days while she searched for a place. She looked around at the house and their old but comfortable furniture. She certainly didn't want to disrupt the boys' lives any more than was necessary at this point. They should definitely stay right here in their familiar surroundings—their home.

At 8:30 a.m., she called Irene, the bookstore manager, to let her know she would not be in today. She tried her best to sound really sick.

"No problem, Amy. You just get yourself back in bed and feeling better!" came Irene's sweet response, which made Amy feel even guiltier than she had before she called.

Amy went upstairs to start packing a bag. What should she take? How much should she take? She felt frozen. Her arm was much better, but still tender. She took some Ibuprofen and then lay down on the bed.

She felt pretty antsy, so after a few minutes, she decided to go back downstairs for a cup of hot tea and to look over the classifieds for an apartment. She couldn't very well pack if she didn't even know where she was going!

It was easier than she thought to find a place to live. Under **Furnished Apartments/Rooms for Rent** Amy had found a private suite with its own entrance priced at $400 a month which included utilities! She could afford that! She could even buy her own mattress and a slip cover for the couch; perhaps some decorations to make the place hers. She called the number provided. The woman sounded very kind, and gave Amy directions. Amy knew the neighborhood. It wasn't too far from here, and it was a really nice neighborhood with lots of rambling, old Victorian homes. She had always admired those houses. She was starting to get excited about the idea! She made an appointment to look at it at noon.

Amy went back upstairs with a new sense of direction.

This is how you get things done, one step at a time!

Then she remembered that she hadn't, after all, told the boys anything on the way to school that morning. She had thought about it, but for some reason just couldn't bring it up. The two of them had been squabbling in the backseat, as they so often did. Amy just hadn't been feeling so sure of her conviction to follow through on this. But she was now. She would tell them when she picked them up from school this afternoon. It would feel more real by then, and she would have something concrete to tell them, like where she would be living. For goodness sake, she would still pick them up from school every day, feed them dinner ... not much would really change for them. Billy would just have to take care of them in the mornings.

Was THAT too much to expect of him?

She and the boys would do fun things on the weekends, activities she had been wanting to do with them, like sledding, story time at the library, and visiting the zoo when it was warm again.

Would they be okay with this?

Why was she feeling so ambivalent?

Billy was an asshole—and if nothing else, I need to teach him a lesson!

She packed enough clothes and toiletries for about a week. She could always get more things as needed. She'd do her laundry along with the boys' stuff when she was here in the afternoons. However, she would *not* do Billy's!

Amy managed to carry her bag down the stairs and then made her way to the coat closet.

She pushed aside the various jackets and winter garments and reached into the very back of the closet for her old coat. She had not added any funding to her stash since before Christmastime, but still had a nice amount to get her by comfortably for awhile.

She felt the empty hanger.

What ...?

She pushed the other stuff further out of the way and saw the estranged hanger gently swinging back and forth without the weight of the coat. She frantically got down on her hands and knees, searching the floor.

What the hell!? Where's my flipping coat?

Her mind was reeling. She searched the other end of the closet, her heart beating faster, her breath whistling angrily through her nostrils.

Okay. Stop. Take a deep breath. Remember, one step at a time.

She slowly and methodically went through every hanging article of clothing, looking carefully between each coat in case she had absentmindedly changed the position of her precious hiding place.

When she was finished—without success—she repeated the process, saying, "No, no, no..." the whole time.

Billy had found the money! Not only found it, but had taken it! STOLEN it! The BASTARD!

She ran to the phone and dialed his office. After the operator put her call through, she could barely contain herself.

"This is Billy Martin. Can I help—?"

"You THIEF!"

"What?"

"Where's my money!?"

"What money?"

"You know damned well. Where is it?"

"I don't know what the fuck you're talking about, Amy."

"Where is my MONEY?" she demanded.

"What MONEY?" he yelled back; then unsure if anyone could hear him beyond his closed door, he repeated in a harsh whisper, "What money?"

By this time, Amy was sobbing. "My savings ... my old coat ... how could you steal it from me?"

Visions spun before Billy's eyes ... of an old coat in the closet and Cassie helping herself to it on a recent cold afternoon ...visions of him watching through the window as she left, the old coat quite snug on her enormous body... Was that the coat Amy was talking about? And what did she mean, *her savings*? What savings? And savings *for what*?

"Amy, I didn't steal *anything* from you. I don't know what you're talking about. What coat? What money? Have you been hiding something from me?"

Amy hung up.

Billy sat there with the receiver still pressed to his ear, stunned.

Yeah ... yeah ... it was all starting to make sense. The bitch had been saving money all along; she was planning to leave him. That was money that should have been used to help pay the bills, and here she was, selfishly setting it aside, hiding it from Billy... so she could LEAVE him?

His mind raced.

How much money was she talking about? Did Cassie have it now? How can I get it back? He glanced at the computer screen and the message from Corporate Human Resources that he had been handling when Amy called. **Annual Benefit Changes/Renewals**, it read at the top of the screen. He had been about to check the box marked **No Changes** and submit it, as he did every year, but at that moment he was filled with rage. Rage at this stranger he had been calling his wife all these years. Rage at her calculation and manipulation. She had been using him! Planning her escape all along—unbelievable!

He thought about Cassie's words: "She wishes you were dead so she could collect your life insurance money!"

He looked again at the screen, noting Amy's name as the beneficiary of his life insurance policy.

He checked the box marked **Cancel**.

There! She can obviously take care of herself and make her own fucking money. I'll be damned if I'm worth more dead than alive to that fucking bitch!

Amy sat on the floor in front of the closet, her head in her hands.

I cannot believe this!

She just knew that Billy had taken her money. She could hear it in his voice when he asked, "What coat? What money?"

He knows damned well what coat and what money! How could I have been so stupid? I should've opened a savings account in my name only. She had considered that, but had been worried about statements coming in the mail. *Should I have gotten a safety deposit box? Oh God! What difference does it make now?*

She called the woman back to cancel her appointment to see the rental. And it had sounded so perfect…

What did he do with her damned money?

She went through his drawers, all the pockets in his pants and jackets. She looked in his shaving kit, then through the drawers in his computer desk. Amy even searched inside his shoes and boots. Nothing. The money was gone. Just gone.

I could KILL Billy!

A half hour later, Amy was knocking on Mom's door.

"Amy!" exclaimed her mother as she questioningly looked at the suitcase in Amy's hand.

"Mom, can I stay with you for a few days?" asked Amy in a quivering voice, tears spilling over her already reddened eyes.

"Oh Amy ... Come in, honey." She wrapped her arms around Amy's shoulders as the suitcase dropped with a thud to the floor. Torrents of sorrow and despair emerged from her eldest and most responsible daughter.

"*Tsk ... tsk ...*" were the sounds that Mom made to supposedly soothe Amy.

Not "There ... there" but, "*Tsk ... tsk ...*"

Ginny managed to stomach Cassie's company during the trek to pick up her car from the salvation yard. Cassie's car was identical to Ginny's: same color and everything. Cassie bought hers after Ginny had purchased hers.

Always trying to copy me ... doesn't she have a mind of her own? What was it they say? Mimicry is the highest form of flattery? Save the compliments Cassie, and get a life.

Well ... the car was one thing ... but as she glanced at Cassie in the driver's seat, Ginny thought, *She obviously doesn't try to copy me in the looks department. But Good God, she should. She's ghastly!*

Ginny's car was drivable. It looked like a piece of shit, but it was drivable. There was dried blood on the steering wheel, seat, and floorboard. Miraculously, the windshield hadn't broken.

Before Cassie left to go back home, Ginny made sure to thank her profusely. She then made Cassie promise not to say anything just yet about what had happened to Ginny or about their plans for an apartment. Cassie agreed and also seemed to be as anxious as Ginny was to get back to her own home. All Ginny wanted to do at this point was to go back to her place, swallow some more Vicodin, and sleep the day away. What was left of it anyway.

~

When Cassie returned home, Mom was upstairs changing the sheets on the bed in Amy's old room.

"What are you doing?" Cassie asked.

"Oh, hi Cassie. Amy needs to stay here with us for a few days. I'm just freshening the room up for her."

"Why does she need to stay with us?"

"She and Billy need a little time apart … marriages go through this sort of thing … ups and downs, you know … it'll be okay …" as she tucked in the corners, ever so neatly.

Cassie just stood there for a moment, thinking,

Jeez, everyone's lives are starting to fall apart. I wonder if the information I gave Billy has anything to do with it, and then asked,

"Well, where is she then?"

"Amy went to pick up the kids from school. She'll do that every day … take care of them, feed them dinner, and then come back here in the evening after Billy gets home."

Cassie noticed that Mom was out of breath.

God! Mom is starting to get old!

Cassie could've offered to help, but she had done enough helping over the past several hours to last a lifetime. Besides, she was tired. She hadn't slept a wink last night.

"So, how is that friend of yours doing?"

Cassie had told Mom that it was a friend at work who had needed her assistance yesterday.

"Oh, she's fine. We just went and picked up her car. She's back home now."

"Well, Cassie, that was so nice of you to do. You can tell me more about this new friend of yours later."

"Oh yeah … sure … I'm just kinda tired right now."

"Of course you are, sweetie. Do you want me to fix you dinner?"

"No. I ate some tacos on the way home. I'm just gonna have a piece of pie and go to bed early."

Mom didn't respond. Instead, she studiously surveyed the

room as she picked up and shook a can of Pledge, then began to spray and wipe down the old but well-cared-for furniture.

Cassie was in the kitchen eating a piece of strawberry-rhubarb pie when she heard the vacuum cleaner start its inward wheeze upstairs. Seconds later, she heard a knock at the side door.

She peered through the glass.

Billy!?

Now it was her turn to rudely ask as she opened the door, "What do you want?"

Billy glanced furtively into the kitchen.

"Quick, Cassie. I need that coat back. Please, just hurry."

"We need to talk, Billy," she said softly. She just couldn't help herself. She should be mad as a hornet at him, especially with whatever monkey business was going on between Ginny and he. But when she looked at Billy, her heart melted. She loved him. She was desperately *in love* with him.

"Damn it, Cassie! I just need the frigging coat. I don't have time to talk, and have nothing to say to you."

Her heart sank like lead in her chest. Her mouth quivered and her hands started to tremble.

She turned, walked to the closet, pulled out the coat, and went back to the door to hand it to Billy. He was impatiently standing with his arm outstretched to grab it from her.

As the coat exchanged hands, Mom appeared in the kitchen doorway.

"Billy? What are you ...?" Then she realized what Cassie was handing to him.

"... and why are you taking that coat?"

"Long story ... gotta go." Billy quickly disappeared, shutting the door behind him.

"Cassie? I thought you said that you got that coat at a thrift store."

"Yeah ... I said that Mom, but I really borrowed it from Amy ... without her permission. I meant to get it back to her before she noticed." Cassie was proud of herself for thinking on her feet like that. She was getting to be a pretty good liar.

But Mom still looked very puzzled.

Cassie quickly said, "I'm going to bed now,"

"But it's so early…"

"I told you, Mom, I'm *tired*!" and she practically ran into her room and slammed the door.

There is something very fishy going on around here, thought Janice.

Before Billy even checked the pockets, he pulled out of the driveway and drove down the street. He parked on the side of the road and then started to dig through the very deep pockets of the coat, until, *Aha!* His hand felt a thick paper envelope with a rubber band wrapped around it.

He slowly pulled it out and turned on the overhead interior light. He removed the rubber band and then lifted the flap of the envelope.

"Holy shit!" he said to no-one in particular.

"Holy SHIT!" he said again.

The bills appeared to be mostly twenties—but there was a huge wad of them!

Billy glanced out the windows into the emerging darkness beyond, and then quickly shut off the light.

He then drove back to work, where he let himself into the empty building, made his way back to his windowless office, and switched on the light.

He sat down and greedily counted the cash. There were fifties, twenties, tens, and fives.

"Holy shit!" he said for the third time when he was finished counting.

ALMOST FOUR GRAND! He had not expected that!

How long has Amy been squirreling away cash?

He looked around his office for a safe hiding place. Nothing seemed secure enough. He grabbed some packing tape from a lower drawer, and went over to the filing cabinet. He heaved it away from the wall, and then proceeded to tape the full envelope to the back of the cabinet. He heaved it back into place.

This was *his* money! After all, Amy was *his* wife, and what was hers was his!

When Billy pulled into their driveway, he felt almost giddy. Amazing what kind of effect money had on him! He had the POWER! Where could Amy go now?

It was destiny for Cassie to have taken that coat.

He couldn't believe she hadn't discovered the cash! If the pockets hadn't been so cavernous … that's probably why Amy had chosen it as a hiding place.

Oh well, finders keepers, losers weepers … HA!

For now, he would just sit on it. As far as Amy knew, he was still clueless about it. He had tossed the coat into the dumpster behind the office building after he had thoroughly rechecked every pocket and fold, hoping to find even more!

It took a little effort, but he donned a morose countenance and entered his castle.

Ginny woke up the next morning and momentarily forgot her predicament, but it all came seeping back as she opened her eyes, blinked back the daylight, and felt the dull ache in her nose.

She went into the bathroom and began pulling the long strands of gauze packing from each nostril. Her nose immediately felt better. She carefully untaped the splint from the bridge of her nose, and then peered out of her slightly swollen eyes at the black-and-blue, disfigured face in the mirror.

"Jesus!" she said to herself.

She jumped as a sharp knock-knock-knock rapped on her front door.

She tiptoed to the door and peeked through the security lens.

There stood Billy, obviously stopping on his way to work, shifting his weight from foot to foot like a nervous bull.

Ginny quietly backed away from the door and knelt behind the wall in the hallway. Her knee landed on a small shard of broken pottery that Cassie must have missed in her half-assed clean-up of the mess she had made. Ginny sucked in a quick breath and reached down to remove the offensive piece.

Knock-knock-knock, came Billy's hard knuckles again.

Damn! She did *not* want him to see her like this.

What is he doing here at the crack of dawn?

Her vanity superceded her curiosity and she remained crouched down and silent.

After several moments it appeared as though he had given up. She crept over to the living room window and looked down. Sure enough, there was Billy getting into his car. He glanced up at her window and she swiftly moved behind the curtain.

She waited a second, and then peered through the blind again. Good! He hadn't seen her. She watched his car slither away, like the snake that he was.

This was all too much! What she had been through in the past few weeks was more than any human being could bear!

Billy didn't love her. He had said as much in the car the other day. Why this came as a shock to her, she didn't know … but it did just the same.

How could he have strung me along all these years? It is unforgivable!

She thought back on when it all started. For crying out loud, she had been a kid. That was predatory behavior on his part—child molestation! Oddly, she was able to forgive Billy more for *that* than for the years of her life he had taken from her.

Her mind drifted to John Gilmore. And *him*! What was it about the men in her life that made them want to lead her on, then just dump her like a sack of shit? That's what she felt like … a sack of shit.

Ginny still could not believe that she had lost her job and possibly her livelihood. Again, she tried to summon up some pity for Mr. Fields, but was incapable of doing so. It was *his* fault that she had lost her job! Why hadn't he been awake when she went into his room? He could've asked, "What's that?" before she hung the bag. She would've said, "Oh, just some penicillin …" And then he should've said, "No, don't give me that. I'm allergic to penicillin."

Could've. Would've. Should've. These three words summed up her life. And now, she looked like a monster … and her car was wrecked.

She needed to call her insurance agent and get the car into a body shop. She was not going to drive a heap of junk around on top of everything else. She shuffled into the kitchen and pulled the phone book out of a drawer.

Hadley … Hadley … ah, there it is, Hadley Insurance.

She picked up the phone and punched in the numbers, glancing up at the clock. 8:30. They should be open. Nope. Voice mail kicked in, so Ginny left a brief, but descriptive message, telling her agent how a garbage truck had pulled out in front of her. She left her phone number so her agent would return her call.

She swallowed some more Vicodin and then went to take a hot bath, where she dipped a washcloth into the water, wrung it out, and carefully draped it over her eyes and nose until it cooled. She repeated the process … It felt good.

The ringing phone startled her out of her reverie. Her answering machine switched on. She heard her greeting: "Hi, this is Ginny. You know what to do!" and then she heard the businesslike voice of her insurance agent. She sat up and strained to hear.

"... and we do hope the truck driver carries good insurance. It sounds as though it was his fault anyway. We are very sorry about your coincidental lapse in coverage, but we have sent two notices that your payment was overdue ..."

What? Ginny quickly stood up, nearly losing her footing. She grabbed a towel and traipsed water from the bathroom to the kitchen, just in time to hear, "Again, we are sorry about your accident. Good luck with getting it worked out." With a click, and then a beep, her machine retained the message.

She stood in the cold kitchen, goose bumps forming on her wet skin, staring at the phone as if it were some alien creature.

"NO ... WAY ..." Ginny shook her head in disbelief, trying to remember if she had even opened those envelopes from her agent.

So much had been going on in her life lately!

She slowly turned her dripping body and headed back into the bathroom, where she mechanically opened the medicine cabinet and pulled down the "goody jar" from Billy. It was over halfway filled with a supply of Vicodin. She carried the jar into her bedroom, then reached into the drawer of her bedside table and pulled out two prescription bottles, one her anti-anxiety meds, the other her sleeping pills. She dumped the contents of each into three piles within the folds of her unmade bed, and then just stared at them for what seemed an eternity.

She imagined herself being found dead as a doornail in her bed by her frantic family after nobody had heard from her for several days ... but wait ... would that make them frantic?

Ginny sometimes went *months* without speaking to her family! Maybe no-one would find her! Maybe she'd just ROT here?

No one loves me. NO ONE LOVES ME!

But no ... Ginny didn't want to kill herself anyway...

She wanted to kill Billy.

Amy was in her childhood bathroom, trying to get ready for work. It was Tuesday and she was looking forward to seeing Geoffrey; though she had toyed with the idea of calling in sick again. She wondered how Billy was managing with the boys …

She had already eaten a hearty breakfast with Mom. She had forgotten what it was like for someone to take care of *her* for a change! Mom had fixed scrambled eggs, bacon, and Pop-Tarts. She had even made Amy some hot chocolate! Amy was beginning to understand how Cassie had fallen prey to this kind of life. Even Amy could get used to it. And it truly seemed to make Mom happy.

She thought about the interchange between herself and Billy, or the lack thereof, when he had finally come home last night. Amy hadn't given him the satisfaction of uttering one word to him. She had been waiting by the door, having put the boys to bed, kissing them goodnight and telling them that she'd see them tomorrow.

Billy had come in with an attitude, as though *he* was mad at *her*. He had some nerve—not that she had expected an apology or anything. That thief had stolen her money … she just knew it! Well, she was not going to let that stop her. In fact, she was even more determined than ever to leave his ass.

She had very calmly and coldly stood up, put on her jacket, and walked right out the door, slamming it behind her.

When she arrived at Mom's, Cassie was already asleep. She and Mom talked a little as Amy picked at the plate of Beef Stroganoff that Mom had kept warm for her. They mostly discussed how the boys were handling this change. Amy assured her that they were fine, at least as far as she could tell. When Amy had told them, they had responded almost as though they'd anticipated it. The only indication Amy had that they were even somewhat concerned was when they asked how long she'd be sleeping at Nana's. They hadn't even asked to come too. She told them that it might be a week or two. At their ages, their minds didn't really look that far into the future anyway.

She suddenly felt a swelling of love for her two babies. She missed the sounds of their rambunctious morning rituals ...

Her absence might teach Billy how to be a better dad. Lord knows, he needed lessons in that department as in countless others.

Mom had seemed a bit preoccupied last night, but that had been just fine with Amy. She was emotionally wrung out and hadn't been in the mood for deep conversation. She needed a good night's sleep, and then some time to just sort things through. Being away from Billy would allow her to think clearly for once.

But, Amy hadn't slept well after all.

Ironically, her childhood bed, which was the same size as the one she and Billy had shared all these years, seemed so small, even having it all to herself! The sensation brought thoughts of *Alice in Wonderland* to mind as she drifted in and out of sleep, dreaming of what was on the other side of the looking glass ...

"You could come live with me."

Amy smiled wistfully at Geoffrey.

"No, really … you could! We could be, like … roommates."

At times, a strange maternal-like feeling would overtake her romantic crush on this young man. She tried to shake it off. She mumbled, "Maybe … but I need some time on my own first."

The idea of moving in with Geoffrey *had* occurred to her, but the more she thought about it, the more inappropriate it seemed. What was going on with her? A week ago, all she'd felt had been desire for Geoffrey. She had thought about him day and night! Now she was feeling … *embarrassed* … about her feelings!

Maybe it was just too much, too soon—or maybe too little, too late?

Geoffrey, young, fresh-faced Geoffrey was looking at her expectantly.

"Geoffrey, this is all overwhelming for me right now. Surely even *you* can understand that … I … I … don't even know which end is up. Please forgive me if I sound dismissive …"

He blinked, looked away, and said, "Uhhh …"

"I'm sorry. I didn't mean to say that …"

Goodness, I'm talking to him like I'm a teacher or something … and he's my student!

"I really just need some time to think. That's all I'm trying to say."

"Of course you do. Of course you do. I understand. Just remember, I'm here if you need me." And then he smiled at her, or at least his mouth had smiled, but not his eyes. His eyes bore the look of hurt feelings.

Amy knew that her words and her tone had caused them. She had sounded so condescending …

Have I been talking to Billy this way all these years?

Cassie had been using any free time she had to look for an apartment for herself and Ginny to share. Cold, hard reality was setting in for her as she discovered just how much her half of the expenses would be. Why would she give up a perfectly good *free* home for one that she'd have to work like a dog for?

It didn't help that Mom was cooking up some great meals these days. Cassie knew that it was in honor of Amy's holy presence; but she enjoyed it all the same.

Amy had been sleeping at Mom's for nearly a week now. It was strange, but life was moving forward and yet standing still. Nobody was talking about the big, white elephant in the room, but no one really knew what that elephant even was. Cassie could sense a feeling of foreboding … for what, she wasn't sure.

Ginny was staying holed up in her apartment. She had phoned Cassie on Tuesday to tell her that once she recovered from the accident, she'd start looking for a place for them. But Cassie had decided to take the initiative. And now Ginny wasn't even answering her phone!

Well, when Princess Ginny got around to either calling or answering her phone, Cassie would inform her sister that it was a *no-go*. Cassie was staying put at Mom's. And she wasn't going to let Amy take over as rooster of the roost either!

Surely, Amy would be moving back home. Cassie wondered what was going on with Billy. She did not want to admit to herself that the possibility of a relationship between he and Ginny existed.

But that phone call … no way! How could Ginny?

Cassie felt a flash of shame. No, it was different for Cassie. She truly loved Billy. He had *used* that love to get what he wanted from her. If Cassie was so willing, then why on earth would Billy go after Ginny? Was Ginny telling the truth when she said Billy was just making fun of her? Cassie really, really wanted to believe that scenario. But, she knew Billy. She thought about his sudden appearance at the house the other night.

Why the hell had he wanted that stupid coat so badly?

She had worried that Mom might mention it to Amy but she hadn't. Perhaps Cassie's story about borrowing it without Amy's permission sufficed to make Mom want to keep the peace between the two of them.

Really, Amy might be sleeping there, but Cassie didn't see her much. Amy was getting into the habit of eating her meal when she got home from her old house, then absconding and wrapping any leftovers to take to the boys the next evening! This done so she wouldn't have to cook for them herself! Lazy pig!

Cassie was just going to bed early every night, watching TV in her room with the door closed until she fell asleep. Not once had Amy suggested that Cassie come out to spend some time with her—not that Cassie even wanted to. Cassie did not like having Amy in her house!

For crying out loud, why doesn't Amy just go out and get her own place? And the boys should really be living with their mother, not their father. In fact, Amy should have insisted that Billy leave the house! More than likely, whatever problems they were having were his fault.

Cassie thought about her sister's wish for instant wealth with Billy's life insurance money.

Maybe I should help her out and just DO HIM IN … the asshole certainly deserves it.

Life was hectic these past few days. Billy couldn't seem to get it together in the mornings, and the boys had been late for school every day. Of course, that meant that Billy was late for work. Even though he was late, he would start each morning by closing and locking his office door, and then counting his money! He then would return it to its hiding place, unlock his door, and tackle his ever-growing pile of claims, glancing from time to time at the file cabinet to make sure it was still there.

This morning, he had no sooner started to work when his boss's secretary buzzed in to inform Billy that his boss wanted to see him at 9 a.m. sharp.

Billy felt the blood drain from his face and a lump form in his throat.

He knew he wasn't up for a promotion, that was for sure! Nine o'clock? That was in fifteen minutes! The Grand Poobah wasn't giving him much time to prepare.

Billy straightened his tie, made sure that his shirt was tucked in and that he hadn't missed any belt loops. He then rubbed his finger vigorously over his front teeth, unsure if he had even brushed them this morning. He tried to appear confident as he made his way to the torture chamber.

He was five minutes early; his boss made him wait until exactly nine before permitting him in. It was an agonizing five minutes … no magazines to look at … just the ticking of the clock and the occasional raised eyebrow appraisal from the secretary.

Finally, her phone buzzed. After picking it up and listening to the caller, she looked at Billy and said, "He'll see you now."

Billy hands were cold and sweaty.

Miraculously, Billy wasn't fired! In fact, his boss had actually been quite nice … very concerned … more so about Billy himself than about the falling behind in his work. Apparently, Billy was very good at his job. His boss had asked what might be done to get Billy "back on his game".

I guess I'm a valuable employee! Heck, maybe I should've asked for a raise! If only Amy had been a fly on the wall, so she could've seen that SOMEONE appreciates me and my hard work!

In order to explain why he had been falling behind, Billy had admitted that he was going through some marital difficulties, and that his wife had not only left him, but had left him to raise their two young sons *all by himself.* His boss had been quite sympathetic, and even offered to divert some of Billy's work for awhile. But Billy had said, "Oh, no. I can handle it. I'll put in some extra time over the weekend." His boss had not argued.

Billy was almost back to his office when he realized what he had done.

Shit! Why did I say that? Damn! I had the opportunity to get out from under that heaping stack of claims, and what did I do? I turned it down! Is it too late to go back and say I changed my mind?

Probably.

He sat down at his desk and began to review claims. He couldn't concentrate. He was surprised Amy hadn't come crawling back home yet. It was only a week, but felt like months. The house was already a wreck. Amy sure wasn't doing much cleaning when she was there in the afternoons. Billy's laundry was piling up; he was shocked at how much clothing could accumulate on the floor of the bedroom in just a few short days.

And by God, he was hungry! Amy fed the boys dinner but did not fix anything for him at all. Billy noticed that the boys had been eating from paper plates ... food that Amy had brought from Janice's, and then heated up in the microwave. But nothing for him! Man! She was really trying to twist the screws. And she was like a racehorse at the gate when he got home at night, practically flying out the door.

He couldn't wrap his head around the idea that she hated him so much. Jesum Crow, maybe she was never coming back. What would he do? How would he take care of things? He was sick to death of eating cereal every night. He didn't know how to cook or clean ... or any of that woman's work crap.

Why does she hate me? Why? What did I do?

Or rather, what did I do that she knows about?

Her behavior was so uncharacteristic of Amy. She was anal-retentive responsible. And now she was just casting off her duties and leaving him holding the bag!

This is not right! Not fair at all.

The first night Amy was gone, Billy had thought, *Fine, I'll just have the house to myself for a while.*

Of course, he had not believed she would be gone more than a day or two. Without Amy taking care of everything, the house was quickly becoming a burden. Nothing but work. And trying to take care of the boys was plain craziness! Billy didn't know what he was doing ... Mornings were absolute *mayhem*. They had been eating school lunches all week, which was great with them, but if Amy knew ... She was convinced that the school cafeteria was rampant with germs. But who had the time to make lunches in the morning?!

Well, if Amy wants to split up, then maybe she should just move back into the house with the boys, and I'll move out. That would make life easier on everyone.

But where would I go?

Maybe I SHOULD just move in with Ginny. Maybe Ginny was right all along. Maybe we belong together. We certainly had some good times over the years ... Yeah! Maybe I should move in with her. That would serve Amy right!

He had called Ginny three times already this week. She hadn't answered. This was nuts! She had never been this mad at him before. He picked up the phone and dialed her number again.

"Hi, this is Ginny. You know what to do!"

Goddamn it, this was really getting old! Ginny absolutely worshipped the ground he walked on; she had *never* treated him like this.

He wished he hadn't said what he had in the car on the day she picked him up from the jail. He had even shocked himself when he heard the words coming out of his mouth. Ginny's face had said it all. Jesus! He was going to have to make it up to her somehow ... if she would just answer her FRIGGING PHONE!

He'd better come up with something, and soon ... and it was going to have to be something good!

He was beginning to feel something uncomfortably familiar, a feeling that he had had as a child ... The very bad feeling that he was slowly being abandoned.

Ginny was going stir-crazy. She had been holed up in her apartment since Saturday, hiding from the world. Her whole life was falling apart. She had used up her entire stash of pain pills trying to numb herself from the ache in her heart and the desperation she was feeling.

On Wednesday, a middle-aged man wearing a tie had knocked on her door. She had reluctantly opened it, but left the chain in place so she wouldn't have to let him in.

"Are you Virginia Miller?" he had asked from the hallway.

"Uh, yeah. But I go by Ginny."

"Here. You are served." He thrust an envelope through the narrow opening, and then he was gone.

Ginny had stood there, turning it over in her hands, as her stomach churned right along with it.

She studied the official-looking envelope, not particularly excited about opening it. It was from the County Sheriff's office.

Her hands trembled as she tore it open.

"What …?" as she skimmed over the document.

Ex Parte/Order of Restraint was printed across the top. "Dr. John Gilmore, petitioner, seeks order of restraint per application/affidavit against Ms. Virginia Miller blah, blah, blah … nondisclosure of location blah, blah, blah … hearing in 14 days blah, blah, blah …"

"What the *hell*?"

She stood in the living room, mouth hanging open, trying to comprehend why John Gilmore had found it necessary to *restrain* her. Was this man trying to totally destroy her? The nerve of that asshole! She hadn't bothered him in any way at all! She was the one who should be taking out a restraining order on *him*! Had that bitch girlfriend of his put him up to it?

This takes the cake.

She walked into the kitchen, ripped the paper into shreds, and tossed it into the garbage can.

I'll stay away from you all right! I won't even show up for the stupid hearing! You'll look like a fool when the person you're trying to get to stay away from you doesn't even show up there! DAMN! DAMN! DAMN!

She was too angry to cry.

With no more pills to comfort her, she went to the closet and pulled down a shoebox containing the large bag of pot and rolling papers she kept on hand.

She rolled herself a fat one and sat in the kitchen smoking it, taking deep, desperate drags until she felt the calming effects. She stubbed out what was left, went into the living room, and flopped down on the couch, staring blindly at the television where an episode of *I Love Lucy* was filling the empty apartment with the sounds of human beings.

How could things get any worse?

Well, they could get worse. Her fuckin' rent was due next week, and she just didn't have it.

She needed help.

She had been ignoring Billy's attempts to get in touch with her, which was getting increasingly difficult as the week wore on. If she hadn't looked so ghastly, she would have answered his calls and opened her door and her heart to him. She missed him terribly. She picked up her phone from the coffee table and could see from caller ID that he had called twice today!

She pulled herself up off the couch, went to the bedroom, and sat at her makeup table, looking critically at herself in the small, table-top mirror. It had been less than a week, but she was healing pretty well. She proceeded to apply makeup, using a concealer to blot away the remaining bruises.

After thirty minutes, she was satisfied with the result. She was almost back to normal!

Picking up her phone again, she dialed Billy's number.

He'd better not give me a hard time about calling his cell because I am merely returning his multitude of calls! He must really miss me … I should have played hard to get a long time ago!

Billy picked up after the very first ring.

"Ginny!"

"Hi Billy." She tried to sound casual and distant.

"Where have you been? I've been trying to call you all week. What's the matter with you? I've been worried."

"Worried? About me?" She was trying very hard to sound carefree, but the tone of his voice and the concern he seemed to be expressing was breaking down her barrier. She suddenly began to cry. Over the phone line, he could tell.

"Ginny … Ginny … don't cry, honey."

She didn't respond. Her still injured nose stuffed up as her crying and distress caused the tender tissue to swell.

"You doht care about be," she managed to say through her tears.

"I do too, Ginny. I really do. I'm sorry about what I said. I didn't mean it, I swear."

Ginny was mad at herself for being so weak.

"Doe … you doht. Hode od …" She set down the phone and gingerly blew her nose before picking it up again.

She had stopped crying. Her self-pity had become indignation. She just knew that Billy meant the awful things that he had said to her. She wished with all her soul that he hadn't. But he had. And she was *not* going to let herself fall into the same old trap. She couldn't. She wanted to—but she couldn't.

At least now there was enough air exchange through her nostrils that she could speak without sounding like a pitiful moron.

"Okay, now I can talk without sounding like Edith Ann.

"Edith Ann?"

"Yeah, you know, from *Laugh In*. The little girl in the big rocking chair? Lily Tomlin's character?"

"Oh, yeah."

There was a moment of silence, which Billy broke.

"Ginny, what is going on with you? Why haven't you answered my calls?"

"You have no idea what I've been going through, Billy."

"That's why I'm asking. How can I know if you won't talk to me?"

"Billy, I've lost my job. I was in an accident after I dropped you off on Saturday. I broke my friggin' nose. I don't have insurance, so I'm stuck with a heap of junk for a car. That asshole, John Gilmore, had the nerve to take out a restraining order on me … on ME! My goddamn rent is due and I'm flat broke. You basically told me that I've been an idiot all these years to wait for you when you had absolutely no intention of leaving Amy. You've USED me … and nothing you do or say can convince me otherwise. I don't know what I'm gonna do, Billy. I don't know what I'm gonna do."

Man! She had thrown a lot at Billy and he was trying to make sense of everything that she had said.

"You had a wreck?"

"Yeah, I had a wreck. Is that the only thing you're gonna respond to?"

"No! No. Are you all right?"

"NO! I AM NOT ALL RIGHT! JESUS! DO I HAVE TO HIT YOU OVER THE HEAD WITH A FLIPPIN' TWO-BY-FOUR?"

She was pushing his buttons, but Billy bit his lip. He *had* to make amends. Here she was, worried about her life … well, he was pretty worried about his *own* life. But he undoubtedly deserved her anger.

"Amy left me," he said.

"I know."

"You know? How do you know?"

"Cassie told me."

"Since when do you and Cassie talk?"

"Well, we're gonna be doing a lot more talking in the months to come."

Christ! That's all he needed, Cassie and Ginny confiding in each other. He could smell trouble coming his way…

"What do you mean? Why would you be talking a lot more?"

"We're getting an apartment together."

"What? Why?"

"Did you not hear me? I don't have a job! I don't have any money to pay my rent! My only other option would be to move back in with Mom! So which one is worse, do ya' think? What choice do I have?"

Billy's mind was racing. This was *not good*. And if Ginny moved in with Cassie, where could he go? With the turn of events in his life, he was now seriously considering moving in with Ginny—it was what she'd wanted for years! He just wasn't sure … But now he was being pushed to the wall. He could *not* allow her to get all buddy-buddy with Cassie. He would be doomed!

He glanced over at the filing cabinet, picturing the fat envelope taped to the back of it.

Reluctantly he said, "What if I pay your rent for next month?"

"And what am I supposed to do after that if I don't have another job yet?"

He stared at the filing cabinet and gritted his teeth.

"Okay, what if I give you enough money to pay for three months? Would you agree to not move in with Cassie?"

"Where are you gonna get that kind of money?"

This was a twist. Billy had never offered to give Ginny money. And Ginny had never asked for it. It would have made her feel like a … a prostitute or something. She had thought about it, that was for sure, but in all honesty had never dared to ask him. But he did owe her … *big time*!

"I've already got it. How much is your rent?"

"You're shitting me."

"No, I'm not. How much?"

He was starting to feel a bit magnanimous.

"Seven hundred dollars a month."

"SEVEN HUNDRED DOLLARS A MONTH? Now you're shitting me!"

Could a stupid apartment really be that expensive? Seven hundred times three … let's see, that was over two grand! Damn!

"I knew you didn't have it."

"I do … I do. It might just take a little time to get my hands on it." Christ! That was more than half of what he had. What was he thinking?

"That doesn't sound like you have it to me, Billy. Why the hell would you offer something that you don't even have? You asshole. You've done this to me my whole life. JUST LEAVE ME ALONE, BILLY!"

She hung up.

Billy was momentarily relieved. He had not realized how expensive apartments could be. Then again, Ginny lived in a pretty nice place … small, but nice. Damn, maybe he should just take his chances and let her move in somewhere with Cassie.

Things were not going well.

He had a headache the size of Texas.

~

Why had she even bothered calling Billy? The nerve of him, offering to help her out with no intention or the means to follow through! How could she have believed him? Even for a minute? She was *done* with Billy! NO MORE!

There was no way out of this. Ginny was going to have move into a place with Cassie after all. Too bad this apartment was so small. It was lucky she was only on a month-to-month lease; although she hated to leave it.

She went to find her little phone book to look up Cassie's cell number. She sure didn't call enough to have it memorized.

She dialed the number.

"Hello?"

Ginny cringed at the sound of Cassie's voice, which strangely enough sounded much like her own. She took a deep breath and tried to sound cheerful.

"Hi, Cassie! It's me!"

"Oh, hi, Ginny. I'm just leaving work, so you've called at a good time."

"Oh, good. How's it going?"

"Fine."

"Good ... uhhh ... have you been looking for apartments?"

Cassie considered telling Ginny that she had changed her mind and was going to stay at Mom's, but then she thought about how Amy was taking over the house and how uncomfortable it was making life for Cassie.

"Well, I looked a little. They sure are more expensive than I thought."

"It won't be so bad if we're splitting all the bills. Did you find anything interesting?"

"Well. I had to work a lot this week ... I didn't have much time."

What is this? Is Cassie trying to get out of it? She should be grateful that I'm even willing to live with her!

But Ginny could not afford to piss Cassie off.

"Why don't we go and look together? We can go out to lunch somewhere and make a day of it! Are you off tomorrow?"

Tomorrow was Saturday, and yes, Cassie had the day off.

Wow! Ginny is sounding as if she really likes me! Maybe this is a good idea! Maybe Ginny and me will become really close, the way sisters should be!

"Yes, I'm off. That sounds like fun, Ginny! What time do you want to get going?"

Cassie's voice had taken on that high-pitched tone, like it always did when she got excited about something.

"I could come by the house to get you and eat breakfast there. But the only thing is, I may want to stop at a couple of places to get estimates for fixing my car ... even though I don't really have the money to fix it right now ... would you mind?"

"Don't you have insurance?"

"Uhhh ... no. I forgot to pay the premium."

"No way." Cassie felt a flood of sympathy for her younger sister. She momentarily forgot her suspicions about Ginny and Billy. In a generous gesture, she offered, "I could loan you the money to fix your car."

"Really? You have money?"

"Yeah! I have a lot of it! I've saved for a long time. I have twelve thousand dollars in the bank!"

Good Lord, maybe I should have just stayed home, like Cassie had all these years ... but then I wouldn't have been able to carry on a relationship with Billy ... It always comes down to Billy!

"That's amazing, Cassie! And I'll take you up on the offer."

It would be awhile before she'd get around to paying Cassie back ... after all, Cassie wouldn't even have that kind of money if she hadn't been taking advantage of Mom all these years! But this was great! At least she could get her car fixed. And Cassie would probably spring for the deposits and the first month's rent ... this may not be too bad.

"Okay, so we'll take your car, stop by a couple of body shops, then check out some apartments and go to lunch! I'll treat!"

Cassie can be very generous …

"Cassie, you're the best!"

Cassie was absolutely glowing with the praise from her wonderful sister! They were going to be roommates and best friends!

Janice put on her favorite Roy Orbison CD, turned up the volume, and set about her weekly housecleaning. There was more work to do now that Amy was back at home, but she didn't mind.

She pondered over the conversations she and Amy had been having every evening. Poor girl, she was so confused about her life right now.

Janice was sure that Amy and Billy would work things out, but she had to admit, having Amy back home was mighty nice.

She dusted the furniture in Amy's old bedroom, hesitating as she wiped down the headboard. How could Amy think this bed was too small or that she was too big for it? It was a very strange thing for her to say, but then again, Amy had just been a young girl the last time she was sleeping in this bed. Maybe that was it.

Janice glanced around the room. It was still pretty darned clean from the thorough job she had done in preparation for Amy's return earlier in the week. Besides, Amy was good about keeping things neat and tidy, unlike Cassie ... what was Janice going to do with that girl?

She made her way downstairs to attack the mess that was Cassie's room. It was amazing how filthy it got in just a week's time.

The first thing she did was gather up Cassie's dirty clothes and dump them in the laundry basket that she had brought down with her. Then she stripped the bed and remade it with fresh sheets. She lugged the full basket back up the stairs to start a load of laundry, and then returned to Cassie's bedroom. She was breathing heavily and her heart beat rapidly; Janice sat down on the bed until she was able to catch her breath.

She then pulled the feather duster from her pocket and started to dust Cassie's electronics, moving to the bookshelf above Cassie's small desk. As she ran the duster across the tops of the books, a title jumped out at her. *Alice in Wonderland* ... yes ... that's what Amy had referred to when she was talking about being too big for her bed. Janice couldn't remember if she had ever even read the book. She reached up and pulled the book off the shelf by its spine. As she admired the beautifully illustrated cover, she noticed the edge of a photograph sticking out from between the pages.

She pulled it out.

What? Oh my! What on earth?!

The photo was a fabrication of Cassie and Billy, with Billy's image taped into place next to Cassie.

Janice was dumbfounded. *What on earth is this?*

She stared at the picture in her hand, suddenly remembering the scene of Cassie handing that coat to a very agitated Billy. When Janice had walked in, the two of them had acted so ... *guilty*.

Another scene crept out from the depths of her memory ... she was returning home from an evening at Beverly's, and as she was coming down the street she saw Billy in his car just leaving her house. He hadn't noticed Janice because he was looking at himself in his rearview mirror, messing with his hair. When Janice arrived home, she found Cassie quite flushed and pretty flustered. Janice had asked her if someone had been there and Cassie had flat-out lied, saying, no, nobody had been there. Janice had always wondered ... and now this.

Just what is going on here? She opened the book and flipped through it. Several more photos fell from between the pages. Janice bent down to pick them up, still not believing what she was seeing.

Why in God's name would Cassie have done such a ridiculous thing? Was she was trying to make it look like Billy and her were a couple? How absurd!

This is troubling. Very troubling.

Could this have something to do with why Amy and Billy have split up? Good God, no ... it couldn't possibly.

Janice tried to imagine Cassie actually taking the time and putting forth the effort to do such an odd thing.

She must have done it that day when she was asking about the box of old photos. But why? Why would she do this?

Janice was totally at a loss as to how to handle this. She put the photos back in the book and continued her cleaning, although in a bit of a daze.

After a few minutes, she returned to the bookshelf and retrieved the photos. She pulled some of the other books off the shelf, shaking them and rifling through the pages. Nothing.

She did not want Amy to see these. And with all her talk lately about feeling like Alice in Wonderland, Janice was surprised she hadn't come in here looking for the book.

Janice went into the living room to turn Roy off, and then took the pictures into the kitchen. She sat at the table and spread them out, looking with disbelief at the images before her.

She looked up at the clock. 4:00 p.m. Cassie wouldn't be home till after five. Amy was bringing the boys to spend the weekend and would be here any minute. Janice had to get rid of these and fast.

She went over to the kitchen closet and popped the lid of the garbage can. She crumbled the pictures, shoving them down into the bag, and then closed the lid.

No, that wasn't good enough.

She pulled the bag out of the can, and even though it wasn't quite full, tied it tightly closed, and took it out to the garbage cans behind the garage; then stuffed the bag into the larger can, pulling another full bag up and over it. *There!*

She went inside, washed her hands, and began to prepare supper.

~

Amy and the boys came clattering into the kitchen a short time later, making a mess of the floor with their wet, muddy boots.

"Bobby! Will! For goodness sake, go take your boots off before you come in!" Janice surprised herself at her outburst. She couldn't remember having ever scolded the boys this way. "It's just that … well, I've been cleaning house all day …" She was feeling irritated for some reason, but that was no excuse for taking it out on the boys.

"Mom, don't apologize. You're absolutely right. Boys, you know better than that," Amy said, with a hint of irritation in her own voice.

"Hi, Mom," she said as she kissed her frazzled mother on the cheek. "Smells good in here."

There was a ruckus as the boys tumbled back into the kitchen in their stocking feet.

"What's for dinner? What's for dinner?"

Janice forced a small laugh. "You boys must have hollow legs! All you think about is food. How does Beef Taco Pie sound?"

"Good!" said Bobby.

"Yeah, real good!" echoed Will.

They ran into the living room where they turned on the TV, arguing over what to watch.

"Good Lord, Mom … they wear me out."

"They're just excitable, Amy. You can't really blame them. Their lives are in turmoil at the moment."

"I know, Mom, I know. That doesn't make it any easier for me, though …"

Janice looked at her daughter. The one who had always seemed to have it all together. The one Janice had never had to worry about. Now, Janice was worried. She was worried about what might be going on that Amy wasn't even aware of.

"Are you okay, Mom?"

"Oh, of course, honey. I just wish I could do something to fix this."

"You can't fix it. It's up to me and Billy to fix it. I just don't know if it isn't too late."

"It's never too late, Amy. Have the two of you talked at all this week?"

"No, not a word. I've been so mad at him, I just haven't wanted to talk. I don't know ... I don't know. Maybe I should just move back home and deal with it."

"I'll tell you what, Amy. Why don't you plan to spend some time with Billy this weekend? You can leave the boys here, with me. Maybe you could plan something nice for the two of you ... and talk?"

"That sounds good and fine, Mom. I just don't *want* to do anything nice for Billy. He does not deserve it, trust me. Life shouldn't be so hard."

"Amy, I know you don't want to hear this, but you two really should consider counseling."

"Mom ..."

At that moment, Cassie walked through the door. As she glanced fleetingly from Amy to Janice, a look of discomfort came over her features; but she put on a smile and said, "Hi! How are things going, Amy?"

The unease did not escape Janice. As she watched her middle daughter remove her coat and hang it in the closet off the kitchen, she again wondered what was going on between Cassie and Billy. Before Amy could answer, Janice told Cassie, "Dinner's almost ready. Why don't you go change out of your uniform and wash up a little?"

"Good idea. I smell like a vat of grease." Cassie giggled as she sidled past Amy and disappeared into the bathroom down the hall.

When they heard the shower come on, Amy turned to Janice.

"Why is she acting so weird?"

"I think she's just acting her usual self, Amy. You haven't spent much time with her over the years."

"Well, why would I, Mom? She's like a Dr. Jekyll and Mr. Hyde. I never know which one she's going to be!"

"Oh Amy, you're exaggerating."

"Whatever ..."

Amy sat at the kitchen table, watching as her mother checked the casserole in the oven, adding shredded cheese to the top of it before shutting the oven door. The warmth of the oven and the mouthwatering smell hit Amy's face and somehow made her wish she were twelve again.

Janice began to get plates out to set the table.

"Why don't you let me do that, Mom?"

"No, honey. I enjoy doing this. You go on and wash up yourself. I know you've had a long day ... but thank you."

"Well, I'm beginning to see how Cassie has gotten so lazy!"

"Amy! What has gotten into you? Cassie is your sister! Why can't you be nice to her?"

"*Aaagghhh* ... fine ... sorry. You should just let us help sometimes."

"I don't need help. But someday I might, and then Cassie will do her share."

"Jeez, Mom! Are you expecting Cassie to live with you for the rest of her life?"

Just then, Cassie walked back into the kitchen.

"For your information, Amy, Ginny and I are getting an apartment together."

Janice and Amy turned to Cassie.

"What?" asked Janice.

"You're kidding," said Amy.

"Why would I be kidding? She's coming over tomorrow morning and we're going to start looking for a place."

Janice and Amy looked at each other.

"Is there something *wrong* with that?" Cassie demanded.

"Well, no, of course not, honey. It's just such a surprise. Ginny has always made it pretty clear that she likes having a place all to herself."

"It was *her* idea! I think she just wants us to be closer."

Amy looked at her sister skeptically; Cassie caught both the look and the meaning.

"Amy, you're just jealous because you're not close to any of us! You're like a stranger. You always think you're better than everyone else!"

"For crying out loud, Cassie! Jealous is the *last* thing I'd be when it comes to either you or Ginny. Look at you both—neither one of you has a life. You're pathetic!"

"Amy!" Janice interrupted.

But there was no need, because Amy abruptly left the kitchen and stomped up the stairs.

"I hate her!" said Cassie loudly enough to make sure that the retreating Amy heard.

"Cassie!" Janice exclaimed.

Why do my daughters treat each other this way?

Cassie went to the oven, opened the door and looked at the golden, bubbly casserole.

"Are we ready to eat?" she asked, as she slammed it shut.

Saturday morning was chaotic. Everyone had plans for the day.

Ginny came over for breakfast; so Janice was surrounded by her three girls as well as her grandchildren. She cooked enough bacon and pancakes to feed a small army.

It was a beautiful day, especially considering that it was February. Although frigid days and more snow were sure to be ahead, this day was like a glimpse of spring. The sun was shining, the temperature mild, and the snow was melting. It had the effect of making everyone feel a bit mad with spring fever.

As Amy tried to assemble the boys for their outing to the library for story hour, followed by a special treat— lunch at Mickey D's and possibly a matinee—she had to practically force them to put on their coats.

"It's *hot* outside!"

"Yeah! It's like *summer*!"

But with the threat of no Happy Meals, Amy won the battle, and out they went.

Next to leave were Cassie and Ginny. They had been chattering excitedly all through breakfast. Janice had watched and listened with a sense of confusion about their sudden thick-as-thieves friendship, especially as it appeared that Cassie was taking control of the situation, while a heavily made-up Ginny seemed to be taking the backseat. Very unusual.

They left in a whirlwind shortly after Amy and the boys.

Janice found herself facing an entire morning of cleaning up the disaster of a kitchen they had left in their wake.

She had an uneasy feeling.

Billy woke up to the sun streaming through the bedroom window.

All was quiet.

Peaceful.

He had the house to himself. It was a strange feeling to wake up entirely alone. Part of him liked it, but another part did not.

When he was sufficiently awake he plodded down the hall to the bathroom, and then downstairs to fix a pot of coffee. His efforts had improved quite a bit, out of necessity.

He impatiently watched as the pot slowly filled with fresh brew; he pulled it out and poured some into his cup before the process was complete. Coffee spilled from the drip chamber onto the hot plate below. It sizzled, creating a burned coffee smell, which Billy inhaled deeply.

He turned toward the kitchen door. The sunlight coming in through the window was blinding. He opened the door, and looked at the snow-covered yard, where splotches of dead grass were becoming visible as the snow melted.

It was really warm out!

He picked up the morning newspaper from the doorstep. It was soggy. He dropped it on the kitchen table as he plopped onto a chair. As annoying as it was that the lazy paperboy hadn't put a plastic sleeve over the paper, Billy was too preoccupied with other things to get upset by a wet paper.

His thoughts drifted to Ginny. He had made up his mind that he would give her enough money to cover two months' rent. Not only would this buy time, but it would buy him the right to stay with her if he needed to. Lately, her behavior had him doubting that she was still as gung-ho about things as she had always been. Something was definitely changing. He was losing the upper hand. Losing his edge.

He hadn't called her back yet to let her know of his generosity. In truth, he was afraid she might hang up on him.

He *had* to win her back over!

This gorgeous day was presenting itself just for his benefit. He could actually plan something at the falls. His wheels began to turn as he poured himself another cup of coffee.

He'd get a bottle of champagne ... no, something much stronger and with a quick and powerful punch. *Jaigermeister*! And he'd bring a nice replenishment for her Vicodin goody jar. Surely *that* would make her happy. And he'd bring his sleeping bag with the waterproof liner ... but ... that was a lot of stuff to lug up the hill.

Hmmm ... maybe he should just go to her apartment. But what if Cassie showed up? Besides, Ginny had a tender spot for the falls. Their best memories were spent up there, lying on the moss, hearing the rushing water ... It was warm enough outside that they could actually get naked and crawl into the sleeping bag! He would give her the money right up front. That way he'd have her gratitude to look forward to.

This was a good plan. No, it was an excellent plan. He had no doubt that she'd be thrilled with it.

He couldn't wait to pitch it to her. He picked up the phone and punched in her cell number.

He was anticipating an enthusiastic response.

"Hi, this is Ginny. You know what to do!"

He bit his lip, pinched the bridge of his nose, took a deep breath, and left a message.

~

Amy led Bobby and Will up the creaky wooden steps to the Children's Reading Room on the second floor. This old library had been here forever. Amy had enjoyed story hour on many a Saturday morning when she was a child. While other kids sat glued to Saturday morning cartoons, Amy had sat cross-legged on the floor with other imaginative children as the grandmotherly librarian read story after story. Amy had been meaning to provide this delight to her sons for some time now.

They were half an hour early. The new, young version of a librarian informed Amy that art time followed story time, when the children could draw pictures of scenes from the story that had been read.

Thus the library would take two hours out of their day.

Amy hesitated and considered a change of plans, but then had a thought. Maybe Geoffrey would meet up with her somewhere nearby while the boys enjoyed the library. They really needed to talk.

She asked the librarian if she was required to stay.

"Oh, no. You can go down to the main floor and do some reading on your own."

"May I leave the premises? Run an errand?"

The librarian looked over at Amy's sons, who miraculously were behaving themselves, pouring over the bookshelves.

"Well, I suppose if you don't go too far and as long as you're back before art time ends ... but I should have your cell number, just in case."

"Of course," said Amy as she jotted her name and number on a piece of paper.

"If I leave the library at all, I won't go far."

She kissed the boys, telling them to have fun and to be good! She then walked downstairs and out the door, breathing in the fresh, damp air and feeling the warmth of the sun on her face. She sat down on the steps and fished her phone out from the bottom of her purse. She knew Geoffrey's number by heart and quickly called him before she changed her mind.

After three or four rings, his answering machine picked up. Amy did not leave a message. She was disappointed, but also relieved.

Across the street was the Coffee House. She bought herself a Cappuccino Mocha and carried it back across to the library courtyard. She sat down at one of the picnic tables and became completely lost in her thoughts as she sipped on her splurge.

~

Janice had finished cleaning the kitchen and then taken a long bath, putting on a velour jogging suit afterward. She sure wouldn't be doing any jogging anytime soon, even if she could! But this was comfortable attire for a Saturday afternoon. She made her way into the kitchen to fix herself a light lunch and heard a peculiar buzzing sound. She glanced in the direction from which it was coming and saw Ginny's cell phone doing a little vibration shimmy across the top of the key shelf. Janice strode across the kitchen and grabbed it before it fell to the floor.

"One new voice mail" read the digital display on the screen.

She couldn't believe that Ginny had forgotten her phone!

Janice stared at the phone in her hand. In small letters under **One New Voice Mail** it instructed her to press Send to retrieve the message.

She pressed Send and then held the phone to her ear.

"Ginny, it's me. I've got the money. I want to give it to you. Please ... *please* meet me at Burkette Falls. I have something special planned for you and me. Something that will make you very happy. I'll be waiting for you there at noon ... Ginny ... I ... ummm ... I love you."

Click.

Janice drew in a shocked breath and quickly placed the phone back on the shelf, as if it had suddenly become scalding hot in her hand.

She tentatively picked it back up to replay it, then quickly and forcefully pressed the End button, as though she could make the phone take it back somehow.

She felt a funny gurgle at the base of her throat that made her want to cough, and a thumpity-thump-thump in her chest. She placed her hand across her heart, breathing hard.

Billy! That was Billy's voice! What is that beast trying to do to my beautiful daughters?!

Her head was spinning as she picked the phone up again. Should she call him and confront him?

She looked at the clock. 11:05.

She tried to remember where Burkette Falls was. It had been ages since she'd been there. In fact, she was just a teenager the last time.

HOW DARE HE?

Janice had always been able to find sympathy and compassion in her heart where Billy was concerned; but he was obviously messing with her daughters. This sort of thing could tear her already fragile family apart! Amy was right. He was *evil* ... pure *EVIL*.

Janice grabbed a jacket, her purse, and a set of car keys, and determinedly set out.

She was going to confront him face-to-face and clear this up once and for all. She stopped short when she realized that Cassie's car was in the driveway, blocking her way out of the garage. She sifted through the keys on the chain. Yes! There was one for Cassie's car on the ring. The girl had misplaced her keys so many times that they had made several copies, putting them in various places in case of an emergency.

She considered moving Cassie's car out of the way so she could take her own, but she didn't have time to lose. She wanted to get to the falls before Billy and was unsure of how long it would take her. She would just drive Cassie's car.

Janice felt frantic and agitated. Her heart fluctuated between a normal beat to a sudden, erratic beat. She did not feel well. But she had no choice; it was going to be up to her to fix this.

She focused her attention on how to get to the falls. She headed north on Highway 100, driving for about fifteen minutes or so.

There! she thought, as she passed a sign with an arrow indicating Burkette Lake would be the next right turn. She would have to make a U-turn and backtrack down the hill to the older, unmarked road that led to the falls. It was all coming back to her now.

She came to a stop at the end of the road. As she opened the door she could hear the waterfalls. She was in the right place.

Now if memory serves correctly, there should be a path. Yes! There it is. Before stepping onto it, she turned to peer up the road. Empty. She glanced at her watch. 11:25. She needed to hurry. He could arrive any minute.

Her feet made crunch-crunch noises as they punched down through the icy crust of snow down to the wet, slushy layer below. She was wearing her canvas slip-ons without socks. It didn't take long before they were saturated and her ankles bright red from scraping against the edges of the top layer.

It felt like an hour of walking before she even reached the base of the upward climb she would have to make.

Am I crazy? This is ridiculous!

She was tempted to turn back around, but thought again of her girls—*all three of them*, somehow being manipulated by this monster. And what had he meant by "I've got the money"? What? Had he robbed a bank or something? At this point, Janice wouldn't put it past him.

Her fury drove her up the path.

Holy Mary, Mother of God! It was a slippery mixture of ice and melting snow. She grabbed at various branches and dead vegetation as she slowly and carefully climbed to the top.

Phew! I thought I'd never make it!

Janice shook uncontrollably as she sat on the big stone at the top. It was colder, much colder, up here on the hill. Not only was Janice chilled to the bone, she was petrified about what she was doing.

What would she say?

How should she act?

What would *he* say?

What would he *do*?

This may have been a very bad idea.

Just then, the sun glinting off a moving metal object on the road caught her attention. She squinted and could just make out that it was a dark-blue car. Billy's car. For a moment, she panicked, because he was expecting to see Ginny's car, but then she realized that her two girls had the same taste … *What luck!*

She felt that annoying gurgle in her throat and the urge to cough. Her heart was banging a crazy beat, like a set of drums out of control. She was having great difficulty catching her breath.

Suddenly she heard a distant crunch-crunch, like the sound her own feet had made only moments ago.

She turned around on the rock to face the other direction and pulled her hood up over her head, as if she could somehow just hide from this inescapable confrontation.

Then she heard Billy's laborious breathing, huffing and puffing, as he made his way to the landing.

She waited without moving an inch as he got his footing.

"Ginny?"

The question in his voice made it clear that he didn't recognize her as the person he had been expecting to see.

Janice shut her eyes tightly for a second, took in a deep breath, and then whirled around to face Billy.

"HOW DARE YOU?!" she spat out.

Billy's eyes opened wide in shock. He instinctively recoiled and stepped backward quickly.

It was the wrong thing to do.

"Oh shiiiiit ..."

He frantically struggled to regain footing on solid ground. This explicative was followed by a very unmanly scream,

"NO-O-O-OOAAAAHHHH ..."

His arms desperately flailed as his body hurtled through the empty, chilled air toward the sharp, icy rocks below.

These would be his final words.

With a *crack* of his skull and *thud* of his body, his life came to an abrupt and premature end.

These sickening sounds were barely audible over the thundering noise of the waterfalls, but she heard them ... loud and clear. They would haunt her for the rest of her life.

As he went over the edge, their eyes had locked. It was the first, and the last time they would actually recognize one another, clearly seeing each other's weaknesses, failures, and sins.

He had seemed to be temporarily suspended ...

But it was just a moment in time, and it quickly evaporated with the mist from the falls.

On hands and knees, she cautiously made her way to the edge of the landing, stunned and absolutely horrified.

It had happened *so fast*!

His limp body seemed to be stuck somehow within the various

rocks below, but his limbs, twisted, broken and bloody, bobbed as if in some kind of funky dance with the churning water.

Janice opened her mouth to scream, but sheer terror paralyzed her vocal chords, resulting in a high-pitched whistle of expelled air.

She suddenly felt very dizzy. She managed to push herself back to the safety of the rock.

The top of her head was buzzing as though she had stuck her finger into an electrical socket. It was an intensely strange sensation. She felt confused, like this was all just a dream … or a nightmare.

Janice wasn't sure how long she sat there with her back against the hard face of the rock. When awareness started to creep back, she realized that she was practically drenched. Sweat?

She edged her backside to where the downward climb would begin, refusing to look over the edge where she knew Billy's dead body lay.

She decided to scoot down, using her heels and grabbing at branches to keep her from sliding down too quickly.

But something was wrong.

Janice had no strength in her left arm at all. It was as if it belonged to someone else entirely. She was frightened, but somehow managed to reach the bottom. She stumbled her way to the end of the road. She was having some difficulty with her left leg as well. The journey was arduous, but she made it.

She couldn't shake the confusion that filled her head. She envisioned brief glimpses of the day's events, but they weren't making sense. She didn't even know that it had all really happened. How Janice drove home, she wasn't sure, but the next thing she knew, she was standing by her bed, shivering.

She struggled out of her wet clothes, suddenly smelling the strong odor of urine, and realized that at some point she had lost control of her bladder.

She pushed her wet, dirty clothes with her right foot until they were hidden underneath the bed, and then managed to work her way into her robe.

~

Cassie and Ginny had not been successful in finding a suitable apartment to share. They had stopped at a couple body shops to get estimates for Ginny's car, which were a lot more than either of them had anticipated. Cassie was beginning to act a bit squirrelly about the money part, even balking at the price of their lunch tab.

It had not gone well; in fact, the day had not brought them any closer. They could hardly wait to get away from each other.

As they pulled into the driveway, they noticed Cassie's car parked at an odd angle and the door to the driver's side wide open.

"What on earth?" said Ginny.

"Who the hell's been driving my car?" asked Cassie.

"Not me!" responded Ginny.

Cassie slammed the door shut as they walked past it.

Just who had the nerve to drive her car? Had Mom?

As they entered the house, an eerie kind of quiet greeted them.

"Mom?" called Cassie from the kitchen.

Silence.

She and Ginny just looked at each other.

"Maybe she's taking a nap … maybe she went to Beverly's and just got tired or something."

"Mom never takes naps. In fact, Saturday afternoon is her favorite time to watch Movie Classics."

Something felt weird. The house was too quiet. Normally, Mom would have started making dinner by now.

"Maybe you're right. Maybe she is taking a nap …" Cassie walked down the hall toward Janice's bedroom.

"MOM!"

Cassie's shriek brought Ginny running. She stopped short at the doorway. Janice was sprawled across the bed, robe wide open for all the world to see her naked, ample, and ghostly white flesh.

Janice heard Cassie's shriek and lifted her head drunkenly in response.

The girls were at her side in seconds, pulling her robe around her and helping her into a sitting position. Her hair was all askew, sprouting out in all directions. Her eyes had a glassy appearance.

"What's wrong?! Mom! Are you okay?!" cried Cassie in her shrill voice.

Janice looked as though she was trying to form words, but nothing emerged from her mouth other than a low moan.

Ginny looked at her mother's face, noting the droopy left eye and downward turn at the left corner of her mouth.

"I'm calling 911! I think she's had a stroke!" Ginny ran to the kitchen to make the call.

Amy and the boys were on their way back when Amy's cell phone rang.

Oh great, she thought, *good timing, Geoffrey.*

When she looked at the caller ID, she realized that it was just Cassie.

"Hello?"

"Amy! Mom's had a stroke!"

"What?"

"Mom's had a stroke! *I* found her! She was on her bed, practically *naked*! She can't talk!"

"Slow down, Cassie! Where is she?"

"She's at Mercy! Me and Ginny are here with her! Oh God, oh God, oh God ..."

"I'll be right there." Amy hung up on Cassie. There was no sense in talking with her when she was hysterical like that.

Amy gassed it in the direction of the hospital.

When she arrived, she was directed to a room on the third floor. She deposited the boys in the family waiting room and then made her way to Janice's room. Ginny and Cassie were both there, hovering over their mother, asking her questions that she obviously could not answer.

"Do you want some water?"

"Are you in pain?"

Amy made her way to the bedside and reached for her mother's hand. She looked at her sister's faces, seeing the fear for their mother in their eyes, realizing how much they loved her. Despite Mom's weaknesses and mistakes, they loved her.

So did Amy.

Amy's eyes welled up with tears as she whispered, "What happened? Where's the doctor?"

Cassie deferred to Ginny, the nurse in the family, to explain it all to Amy.

Mom had had a CT scan, and it was pretty certain that it was an occlusive stroke, which meant that it was caused by a clot. She was also in a heart dysrhythmia called Atrial Fibrillation, which was probably the reason that the clot had formed in the first place. Since they didn't know for sure when the stroke happened, they decided not to use a clot-buster, but instead put her on an IV drip of Heparin, which was a type of blood thinner. The heart problem was intermittent; they were giving her a drug called Digitalis to try to keep it regular.

A lot of this went over Amy's head. "Aren't they going to do something to help her?" she asked Ginny.

"They're doing everything they can right now, Amy. It's kind of a time-will-tell situation. She may improve over the next few days, and they'll determine what she needs then."

"Well, I want to talk to the *doctor*. Where is he?" replied Amy as she dismissed Ginny's explanation.

"Suit yourself. He said he'd be back to do rounds at about six."

Amy wanted to stay at the hospital with her mom, but couldn't expect the boys to hang out in the hospital waiting room all evening. She told them that Nana was sick, but that she'd get better. Then she tried to call Billy at home, at work, and on his cell phone. He wasn't answering.

Her blood boiled at the thought of him ignoring her phone calls.

Who the hell does he think he is?

After trying to reach Billy for an hour, to no avail, Amy asked Ginny if she would take the boys back to Mom's and order pizza and keep them distracted with movies. Ginny didn't have to be asked twice. She was greatly relieved to be leaving. She had been deathly afraid of running into John Gilmore, and just plain didn't feel comfortable in her old place of employment. Who knew what rumors were being spread about her?

Cassie decided to retreat as well. After all, there was nothing she could do, and Amy was staying. Mom was pretty much just sleeping anyway.

Not much later, the doctor came by to check on Janice. He practically recited the very same information Ginny had told Amy earlier, but somehow it held more authority coming from him rather than Ginny. He asked Amy if she had any questions, but she was unable to think of even one. She was exhausted.

The nurse and the nurse's assistant each came in at intervals to check on Janice. A speech therapist attempted to feed Janice something that looked like baby food. With each small mouthful Janice managed to swallow, the therapist said, "Good job!" as though Janice actually was a baby. Amy found this difficult to watch; so took this time to find her way to the cafeteria, where she bought a stale-tasting tuna fish sandwich and a carton of milk.

She took her time eating and watching as medical personnel, family members, and even some patients wearing robes over their hospital gowns took advantage of the evening break ritual called dinner.

By the time she returned upstairs, her mother had been toiletted, bathed, and changed for bedtime. *Was there actually a bedtime if you always stayed in bed?* Amy wondered.

She also wondered what might be going through Janice's head. It was so hard when you couldn't communicate to ask how she might be feeling ... what she might need.

Seeing Mom like this made Amy feel particularly vulnerable. Her mother had always held things together and never needed anyone or anything—except for Chuck. It had been so different when Dad was alive. Back then, Janice had always deferred to Chuck. Back then, Amy had seen her as a helpless weakling. The only thing that Mom had under her control was the housekeeping, and she had grabbed onto that like a lifeline. Maybe that was why she had never been able to let her daughters take over any of that stuff. How sad.

Amy jolted awake for no apparent reason. She had somehow drifted to sleep in the stiff, uncomfortable chair next to Mom's bed. The room was only semi-dark, with built-in nightlights by both the entry door and the bathroom door. Plus, the bright lighting in the hallway crept under the threshold of the door with some intensity. It wasn't exactly conducive to a good night's sleep. But Janice was dozing away.

Amy picked her purse up off the floor and carried it into the bathroom. She pulled her phone out, scrutinizing the screen to see if Billy had tried to call her back. Nope. *That shit!*

She called him again at home and the answering machine picked up with her own recorded voice. She hung up and tried his cell phone, then his office. Both went to voice mail.

Where the hell is he? Out partying? On a date with some floozy? He sure isn't wasting time, is he?

Despite the anger, an uneasiness was creeping in at the edges.

Sunday turned out to be another unseasonably warm day. Bobby and Will were busting at the seams to go home and get their bikes so they could go out riding. Ginny promised them that she would take them after lunch. She wanted to give Billy another opportunity to make her some kind of offer. Things weren't looking too good as far as her and Cassie getting a place together, and even if they did, it probably wouldn't take long before one of them killed the other.

It was just *not* a good idea for them to live together.

She was pouring herself a cup of coffee when Cassie emerged from her bedroom. Ginny did a double-take. It was a toss-up whether Cassie looked worse first thing in the morning or totally made up in the freakish way she insisted on wearing her makeup. But as Ginny observed the face of her older sister while Cassie poured herself a cup of coffee and pulled out a chair to heave into, she was suddenly struck to find some resemblance to her own face. If Cassie lost some weight and grew her hair longer and used makeup the way it was intended, for God's sake, she might just *not* be so bad looking.

"What?" asked Cassie when she became aware of Ginny's scrutiny.

"Oh, nothing. I'm just … spacing, I guess."

"Hmmm …" as Cassie sipped her coffee, then,

"I still can't believe that Mom had a stroke. Have you called Amy yet this morning?"

"Yeah, I called her first thing. Nothing's really changed."

They sat in silence for a few minutes.

"Where's Will and Bobby?"

"They're outside. I don't think they quite know what to do with themselves without their video games. And there's nothing for them to watch on TV."

Cassie peered out the kitchen window.

"Gosh, it's another gorgeous day. This is so weird!"

"Yeah, too bad it's under these circumstances. Makes it hard to enjoy."

"Have you guys eaten breakfast?" asked Cassie.

"No, we were waiting for you to get up."

This small act of courtesy brought a smile to Cassie's face.

"What?" asked Ginny.

"It's just nice that you waited for me."

"Oh, no problem ..." Ginny smiled back at Cassie.

The tension that had built up between them the day before suddenly eased up.

"So, what's the plan for the day?"

"Well, Amy wants to stay at the hospital with Mom. I'm gonna take Will and Bobby back over to their house this afternoon. I'll probably just leave them there with Billy, and then go back by the hospital."

Cassie thought about asking Ginny if she wanted her to tag along, but the thought of seeing Billy was not an appealing one. Cassie just knew that her suspicions were indeed fact. As much as she didn't want to admit it, she was sure there was something going on between Ginny and Billy. She had been thinking about it all night, vacillating between righteous anger, abject humiliation, before finally succumbing to resignation. Her flight of emotions throughout the night had left her completely drained of them this morning, which was probably a good thing. She had *almost* woken up Ginny in the middle of the night during a moment of fury, but now she was glad that she hadn't. Cassie just wanted to understand. Why would Billy have messed around with Ginny when Cassie had done everything for him? She would have done anything he had asked.

Ginny was sitting and staring vacantly out the window.

"Ginny ... can I ask you a question? And would you promise to be really honest with me? I swear, I won't freak out."

"You won't freak out? What's that supposed to mean?"

"I just need for you to be *really* honest with me, and however you answer, I won't get upset."

"Uhhh ... okaaay. What?" But it was as if as soon as she said okay, she realized what Cassie was going to ask her about. And she was right.

"Do you and Billy have something going on?"

Ginny opened her eyes wide and looked at Cassie with that feigned incredulity that someone takes on when they want to deny something that they know darned well they are guilty of. And what was more, Ginny knew that Cassie knew. But she adopted the look just the same.

"Cassie! I TOLD you already—"

"Ginny ... don't lie." Cassie's tone was calm. There was no doubt that she already knew the truth.

For a moment, Ginny looked like a terrified, wild animal caught in a trap ... but then her countenance crumpled in upon itself, and she broke down, sobbing.

Little did either of them know that this was the only response Ginny could have had at this point that would work to keep Cassie's emotions in check.

Ginny's pain was evident, and honestly, seemed to be much worse than any pain that Cassie had endured due to Billy's preying indiscretions. Ginny's sobs were wretched and they rendered her speechless. She was heaving, choking, sputtering ... as Cassie watched. It seemed to go on for an eternity. Cassie glanced anxiously outside for any sign of the boys.

Finally, Ginny's torrent of emotions lessened to a hiccoughing, slightly more controlled version of anguish. Her nose had started to bleed, and her tears had smudged her make-up so that the black-and-blue remnants under her eyes were visible. She looked utterly pitiful.

"I ... I ... I've thought about ... just ... just ... *killing* myself!"

Cassie handed Ginny a paper towel for her nosebleed, but after she handed it to her, she bent down and wrapped her arms around Ginny's shaking, skeleton-thin shoulders.

This show of compassion brought another flood of tears. Cassie held Ginny through it, murmuring, "It's all right. It's gonna be all right."

At some point, Cassie refilled both of their coffee cups and sat back down.

The way that the whole story erupted from Ginny, it was a wonder that she had been able to keep any of it in for all these years. The words stumbled and tumbled out of her mouth. She talked for over an hour.

Cassie was incredulous. Seeing the pitiful result of Ginny's miserable life had the same effect of pouring cold water over the coals of any remaining embers of anger. Ginny went on and on and on, punctuated by moments of emotional devastation. It was impossible not to feel sorry for the girl.

When it finally appeared that she was spent, Cassie quietly said, "I can't believe you have been keeping this to yourself all these years. What a … an unbelievable *burden*. Ginny … poor, poor Ginny. I wish I could have protected you somehow."

Cassie was feeling a tiger-mother instinct kicking in. Her hatred of Billy had somehow multiplied a hundred-fold. She still felt her own self-pity, but for some reason was no longer confused by feelings of longing for Billy. In fact, she was completely disgusted at the thought of him. She was cured! Unfortunately, at Ginny's expense … But no, what happened between Billy and Ginny had nothing to do with Cassie.

The pain that Ginny had suffered for *so long* because of Billy somehow prevented Cassie from feeling even an ounce of the jealousy she had felt when she was merely suspicious of the two of them. Now, she felt entirely protective of her baby sister. And she was seeing poor Amy's life in a different light as well. She wondered if it might help Ginny to know what a total rat Billy *really* was.

She hesitantly ventured,

"He seduced me too, Ginny," in a quiet whisper.

Ginny looked up, dazed.

"What?"

"Oh! Not like you at all … and it was just a few times—"

"WHAT?!"

Ginny's face went from a splotched purplish-red leftover from her physical upheaval, to quickly draining of all color. She suddenly looked as though she might pass out.

"No … no. No." she said under her breath, shaking her head.

Then she suddenly stopped, stared at Cassie with overly bright eyes, and said,

"Why would you say that, Cassie? *You're lying.*"

"Ginny, I'm not lying. Why do you think I went totally berserk at your house when he called you that day? I had thought, up till now even, that I was in love with him."

The slap that came across Cassie's face was quick and sharp. She was too stunned to move as Ginny jumped up, grabbed her car keys, and flew out the door. Her face stung vibrantly, and her eyes watered from the pain.

She heard Ginny's car roar to life, then the screeching sound of burning rubber as Ginny tore out of the driveway and down the street.

Ginny pulled into the driveway at Billy and Amy's house. She had the car door open before she had even come to a complete stop. She ran to the front door and began pounding on it with both fists, intermittently yanking on the handle and shaking the door. When there was no answer she quickly went around back, repeating the banging and shaking on the kitchen door.

It became apparent that Billy wasn't home.

Or was he there, but just hiding from her?

Ginny turned, searching the yard for something to break a window with. There was a medium-sized clay pot by the side of the door. She picked it up and smashed the glass window of the door, and then pushed the shards out of the way so she could reach in and unlock it.

She immediately began to scream Billy's name as she entered the house, on a frantic search for him. She was totally out of control, much like Cassie had been on the day that Billy had called and Cassie had answered.

Ginny was shoving dishes off the table and counter to the floor. As she moved into the living room, she tipped over tables and lamps, pulling curtains down, all the while screaming Billy's name.

She didn't even hear the loud knocks on the front door, followed by the hard kick as it was busted down, and two policemen entered with guns drawn.

"POLICE! STOP WHERE YOU ARE AND PUT YOUR HANDS OVER YOUR HEAD!"

Ginny stopped, turned toward the police, and tentatively held her hands up, palms facing forward.

What the hell?

"This is my *sister's* house," she desperately began to explain, as her hands drifted back down to her sides.

"KEEP YOUR HANDS OVER YOUR HEAD!"

Ginny did as she was told, but responded with, "What on earth? I told you, this is my *sister's* house ..."

"What are you doing here, ma'am?"

Ginny again started to put her hands back down, unsure of how to explain the answer to that question.

"PUT YOUR HANDS BACK OVER YOUR HEAD!"

Now Ginny was mad.

"What the *fuck*? You want to know what *I'm* doing here? Well, what are *you* doing here? I told you, *THIS IS MY SISTER'S HOUSE!*"

At this outburst, one of the officers approached Ginny and quickly and expertly handcuffed her wrists behind her back.

"WHAT ARE YOU DOING?" she wailed.

"We are taking you in for questioning related to the murder of William Martin. You have the right to remain silent ..."

Ginny's mouth hung open, her eyes wide and unseeing as they recited her Miranda rights. *This wasn't happening. Murder? Billy? No ... WHAT?*

She was silenced by her shock.

They escorted her out the door and pushed her into the backseat of the cruiser.

She finally found her voice.

"What are you doing? What are you *talking* about?" she demanded.

"Can you tell us where your sister is, ma'am?"

"Why? She's at the *hospital*!"

"The hospital? Is she hurt?"

"What's going on? Where are you taking me? Where's Billy?"

Ginny's thoughts were in chaos, irrational and scattered. She could barely form a sentence.

It hardly registered as she heard the officer call Dispatch to send a unit to Mercy to locate the deceased's wife.

Deceased? What are they talking about?

"WHERE'S BILLY?!" she screamed.

"Calm down, ma'am. You'll be questioned at the station."

After witnessing Ginny's display at the home of the victim, or possibly victims, there was no doubt in the policemen's minds that they had their killer. The only question was, had it been on purpose, or was it an accident?

~

Amy was startled by a quick rap at the door, followed by its opening before she could even say, "Come in."

The nurse had an anxious look on her face as she told Amy, "There are two police officers here asking for you."

"Police? What for?"

"I don't know."

Amy stood up, befuddled. She couldn't imagine what the police would want. She followed the nurse to the nurses' station.

"Are you Mrs. William Martin? Amy Martin? Residing at 24 Walnut Street?"

"Uhhh ... yes."

Good Lord, could this have something to do with that stupid domestic altercation between Billy and me?

"When was the last time you saw or spoke to your husband, ma'am?"

"Ummmm ... Friday? ... Friday afternoon, briefly, when I picked up my kids. We're, ummm ... separated at the moment."

The cops looked at each other, and then noticed the nurse hovering within earshot.

"Is there a private room we could use to speak to Mrs. Martin?" one of them asked the nurse.

The nurse reddened as she said, "Oh, yes. Right this way." She led them to an empty family waiting room.

One of the two officers gently took Amy by the arm, as though he were escorting her on a date or something.

When they were inside the room and the door was shut, Amy sat down on one of the chairs that lined the wall. She quickly stood when the officers remained standing.

"No, please sit down," said the officer who had held her arm. He had a kind face, but he wasn't smiling. Amy was confused.

He sat down next to Amy as she took her seat again.

"Mrs. Martin, I'm afraid we have some bad news. Your husband, William—"

"Billy ... ummm ... he goes by Billy."

"Billy was found at the base of Burkette Falls this morning by two young boys. I'm so sorry to tell you, he was found dead at the scene."

Dead? Billy? Burkette Falls?? The officer's words echoed in her head, but her mind was blank otherwise.

Amy felt nothing. What on earth was the matter with her? How could she feel nothing? She had just been told that her husband was dead! How does someone act in this situation? Should she cry? She sensed the two officers looking at her, waiting for a response of some kind.

She managed a pained, horrified expression, but the tears wouldn't come. Was she in shock?

What the hell is the matter with me?

The officers continued to look at her, exchanging glances with each other as they waited for the news to sink in.

"How … when … Are you sure?" she faltered. And then, gratefully, she felt herself slipping into unconsciousness.

As Amy came to, her mind was fuzzy on the recent facts that had been thrown at her. Was it just a dream?

But, as the room came into focus and she saw the same nurse's anxious face hovering just inches away and two distinct blue masses just behind her, which could only be the blue of police uniforms, Amy realized that, no, she had not been dreaming.

She attempted to sit up, but the nurse gently kept her from doing so.

"Don't get up too quickly. Just take some deep breaths. Let me know when you're ready and I'll help you."

"I'm ready now." Amy accepted the assistance and worked her way onto her feet.

"It's a good thing you were sitting when you passed out. This officer here actually caught you before you hit the floor!"

Amy looked up at him and gave a half-hearted smile.

"Thanks," she said.

The nurse scurried out to get some ice water and Amy resumed her position in the same chair.

"Do you remember what we just told you, Mrs. Martin?"

"Yes. Yes ..." Now the tears came, her thoughts suddenly turning to Will and Bobby. She covered her face with both hands.

"Do my sons know yet?" she asked in a muffled voice.

"No, ma'am. Not that we know of. Where are your sons?"

"They're at my mother's house." Her tears were already starting to dry up, but she kept her face hidden by her hands. Oddly, something within her wanted to smile. The reflex was completely involuntary. It was inappropriate, and she was ashamed. *What the hell is wrong with me?*

The nurse came back with the water; Amy held one hand up as if to say, "Not now" while she tried to pull herself together and control her ridiculous expression.

Finally, she rubbed at her eyes and lifted her head. She took the water and gulped down half the cup. "Where is he? Can I see him?"

The officers looked at each other uncomfortably; then the nice one replied,

"Actually, he's here in the basement, the morgue. We would like for you to make a positive identification."

"You mean it might not be *him*?" she asked, confused again.

"Oh no, it is definitely him. We identified him by his driver's license and one of the officers at the scene knew him personally. But we are required to have a family member ID him as well."

"Oh. Of course ... so can I see him now?"

"Are you up to it?"

"Yes. Yes, I want to."

They made their way down to the morgue. As Amy walked through the corridors, flanked by the two policemen, she felt strangely guilty. She kept her head down as they passed the various nurses and patients. Thank God the elevator was empty as they descended to the ground floor.

She was eager to see Billy's body. Maybe that would make it more real to her, and she would actually *feel* something.

The room was cold. Freezing, in fact.

Billy's was the only body laid out and covered by a white sheet on one of the several stainless-steel gurneys that lined the wall.

Amy's teeth chattered as she was led in by the nice cop, who had finally introduced himself as George McKenna.

As they stood at the head of the steel gurney, Amy glanced down and saw Billy's unmistakable feet, middle toe much longer than any of the others. Amy had often laughed at him because of that obnoxious toe. A string was tied to one of the big toes, the one on the right. There was a tag attached that had numbers and what looked like a date written on it. She felt like she was watching a movie or something.

She was still staring at the toe tag as George pulled down the sheet just enough to reveal Billy's face.

Amy turned her head in that direction, but it was as if she were immersed in water, the movement somehow muddled, slowed.

This can't be real!

His eyes were closed, but his eyebrows were raised, as if surprised at his own death. His mouth appeared as if it had been forced shut, lips barely apart—and blue. There were traces of dried blood at the corners of his mouth and around his ears. His skin color was a ghastly whitish-gray. Only his hair looked alive. He *still* had great hair. She noticed a few strands of gray at his temples, but the rest was still shiny black and thick against the cold, hard tray. She tentatively reached out to touch his hair, but George grabbed her hand before she made contact.

"I'm sorry, this is still under investigation. Right now he is considered … evidence. I'm so sorry. This is your husband then? William Martin?"

Amy's eyes swept to the side to look at him, not really comprehending.

"Yes, this is Billy." Then she turned to walk out of the room. She was in a daze. George quickly flipped the sheet back over Billy's face and got to the door before Amy, opening it as Amy absently walked through. He took her by the arm again as they walked down the hall toward the elevators.

"I need to go to my sons."

"Would you like for us to take you?" asked the other cop, who had been waiting in the hallway.

"No. No thanks. I'm okay. I need to tell them … I need to be with them."

"Are you sure you're okay?"

"Yes, I'm fine. Did you say Burkette Falls? Why was Billy at Burkette Falls?"

"We don't know, which is why we'll need to get some information from you. But we can do that later today. Can you please give us the address where we can reach you?"

Amy wasn't sure where she'd be, but at this point she just wanted to go home—her home. She told them that was where she would be.

Will and Bobby's stomping feet and excited voices broke the icy silence that surrounded Cassie as she sat frozen at the kitchen table.

"Man! Did you SEE that?"

"Aunt Ginny is CRAZY! She drives like Mario Andretti!"

Cassie tried to look normal as they entered the kitchen.

"What was wrong with Aunt Ginny?" asked Bobby.

"Oh," said Cassie with a pasted-on grin, "she was just running late … for something …"

"Work?" asked Bobby.

"Church?" asked Will simultaneously.

"Uh … no. Definitely not church …" Cassie trailed off.

"Are you guys hungry?" she suddenly asked.

"You betcha!"

Cassie smiled at the boys. They were so cute! She was going to make them something special.

"Can you guys set the table and pour us some juice?" she asked as she dug around for a frying pan. "I'll make some bacon and French toast."

Cassie was relatively uncomfortable in the kitchen, but her maternal instincts were emerging. She had often thought about having children of her own but getting a husband hadn't exactly presented itself to her. She tried to imagine if Will and Bobby were her sons, her and Billy's …

Damn! It was so easy to fall back into that way of thinking. Billy is a loser!

He had used her, and he had used Ginny! How could she forget that so easily?

Poor, poor Amy. Cassie wondered if she had a clue. Knowing about Ginny somehow made Cassie feel less guilty about her part in the deception … in fact, she just might tell Amy about *all* of it, including what she now knew about Ginny. After all, Amy had a right to know. She should *want* to know if she is being made a fool of! She was already in the process of leaving Billy … and this might be just what she needs to justify divorcing him … then Billy would be free! Would he choose Cassie?

She just couldn't help herself—and being here, taking care of the boys … it *could* happen!

They ate their breakfast together at the kitchen table, laughing as they talked about boy things, like burps and farts. After breakfast, the three of them watched *Jaws*, which happened to be one of Cassie's favorite movies. By the time the movie was over, the boys were *starved* again!

"I guess Nana must be right about you guys, you do have hollow legs! You wanna make ice cream sundaes? It sure is like summer already, so we might as well celebrate it!"

Cassie was trying really hard to be the perfect mother figure. It was fun to pretend.

They were having a grand old time making a total mess of the kitchen when Amy appeared in the doorway. She looked like hell, and she just stood there, looking at them in a strange way.

For a moment, Cassie panicked, wondering if Amy somehow knew her thoughts …

Then Amy spoke. "Will … Bobby. I need to talk to you guys."

She sat down heavily in one of the empty chairs.

"This is YOUR fault!" cried Bobby as he jumped up, knocking his chair over.

Will sat still, tears filling his eyes, his jaw quivering.

Cassie stood up.

"*What?*" she asked, incredulously.

Bobby ran outside, slamming the door behind him.

Cassie went for the door. "I'll go, Amy. You stay here with Will."

Amy was at a loss. Bobby's response had thrown her. How was this her fault?

Will's shoulders had begun to shake. He put his head down on the table and began to beat his forehead on its surface.

"Will, stop. Honey, please …"

Amy moved her chair over so she could wrap her arms around her eldest child.

"How … how … how did it ha … ha … happen?"

"We're not sure, honey. He may have slipped or something."

"Why was he *there*?"

Amy didn't know. What could she say to her grieving child? She wanted the answer to that question as well.

"I don't know, honey. I don't know. "

The kitchen door opened; Cassie and Bobby came back inside.

Bobby wouldn't look at Amy. He stared at the wall above her head.

"Bobby … honey. Come here." She reached her arms toward him.

"NO!" He bolted down the hall and up the stairs.

"Maybe you should let him process this, Amy," advised Cassie.

"What do *you* know?" responded Amy, but she stayed put, torn between trying to comfort Will, who was sobbing almost silently, still banging his forehead on the table, and Bobby, in a self-imposed emotional exile.

"Will … *STOP!*"

He sat upright, looked her in the eye, and shouted, "Bobby's *right*. It *IS* your fault! You shouldn't have left Dad. This wouldn't have happened if you hadn't left us!" He jumped up and followed in his brother's footsteps.

Just then, the telephone rang. Cassie hesitantly picked it up.

"Hello?" she said in a weak voice.

She listened for a moment.

"A lawyer? That's crazy," she said, glancing nervously at Amy.

"What?" asked Amy.

"Uh, hold on, Ginny." Cassie covered the mouthpiece with her hand and spoke to Amy.

"Ginny's at the police station. She's being questioned about ... about ..."

"Billy?" Amy finished.

"Yeah. And she wants me to call a lawyer."

Now Amy was REALLY confused.

"Tell her I'm coming down there," she told Cassie.

"But what about the boys?"

"If I don't go down *there*, the police will be coming *here* to ask me questions. I don't want the boys to see that. You take care of them. ... Please, Cassie. They don't want to talk to me right now anyway."

She grabbed the phone out of Cassie's hand. "Look Ginny. I don't know what's going on, but I'm coming down to the station to find out."

She hung up.

Amy stood silently, looking at Cassie for a minute; then picked up her keys and walked back out the way she had come in.

Amy couldn't believe the police wouldn't let her see or talk to Ginny. What was worse was that they refused to even tell Amy why Ginny was there in the first place, and why she was being held. Apparently, not only did Ginny need an attorney, but that attorney would be the only person allowed to talk to Ginny.

Amy was ushered into a back room at the station where a pot of coffee was brewing. A female officer by the name of Shelley O'Conner was assigned to question her. She started by offering Amy some coffee. When Amy declined, she took a seat at the desk across from where Amy had been seated.

"I just have a few questions for you, Mrs. Martin," she began.

Amy interrupted with, "What on earth is going on here?"

Shelley continued as though she hadn't heard Amy, "As I said, I have a few questions for *you*, Mrs. Martin."

Amy stared at her blankly. This was crazy.

"You stated that you last saw your husband on Friday. Would that be February 8th?"

"Uhh ... yes. I guess so. I mean, that's right ... Friday, February 8th. I was picking up my two sons for the weekend."

"Yes. And you stated that you and your husband are currently separated?"

This question made Amy feel very uncomfortable, like just because she and Billy weren't getting along that she was a *suspect* or something.

"Yes, that's right. But we would probably have worked things out. It was just temporary."

"Had your husband contacted you to meet him at the landing at Burkette Falls? To work things out, maybe?"

"What? No. Why would he do that? If he wanted to talk, we would have talked at home. Why was he even there?"

"Well, that's what we're trying to figure out, Mrs. Martin."

"You and me both ..."

"So, you did not see or speak to your husband any time after Friday, February 8th?"

"No! For God's sake! No! In fact, I called him several times on Saturday night, after my mother had her stroke—but he never answered."

"Can you tell me where you were and what you did on Saturday, February 9th?"

"You want to know where I was all day? Why? Am I a suspect? Is Ginny a suspect? Why is she here? Why can't I see my sister?"

"Please, Mrs. Martin. This is just a formality at this point. We need to know where you were and what you were doing."

Amy relayed the events of the day as best she could. She left out the part about going for coffee and sitting out in the courtyard for as long as she did. It was inconsequential anyway …

The cop must have been satisfied with her explanation, but then she moved on to questions about her and Billy's relationship.

This new line of questioning made Amy feel even more ill at ease, and her face became flushed as she fidgeted in her seat.

"We're like most married couples, I guess. I mean, sure, we fight sometimes, but nothing major."

The cop interrupted her as she removed a form from the folder in front of her.

Jesus! It's the stupid police report from the night I called 911!

"Can you tell me what happened between you and your husband on Friday night, February 1st?"

~

Amy breathed a huff of nervous exhaustion as she finally exited the station. Why did she feel guilty? She hadn't done anything!

She had glossed over their marital discord, and had actually laughed self-consciously as she tried to shrug off that awful fight she and Billy had had. Did that cop think she was somehow involved in what happened to Billy?

Why the hell had he been at the falls? And what the hell did Ginny have to do with any of it? Amy actually pinched herself, *hard*, to make sure this wasn't a nightmare.

The only thing Amy had been able to find out in regard to why Ginny was being held was that they had discovered her at Amy's house in a state of complete insanity. The cop told Amy that Ginny was in the process of tearing the house apart when the police had arrived to inform Amy about Billy's death.

This did not make any sense.

Amy decided that before she picked up the boys, she would stop by the house to clean up any mess that Ginny had made.

She was unprepared for the devastation in her home. She numbly went about picking up the ripped curtains, the broken furniture and knick-knacks, sweeping up broken glass … it seemed to take hours. It was as if the Tasmanian Devil himself had tornadoed through!

Amy couldn't bring herself to finish the job. It was just too much. She sat down on the living room couch and felt immobilized. Her thoughts scattered from one recent event to another, trying to make some sense of it all. Her mind went back to Thanksgiving and her own venomous words, wishing her husband dead. She hadn't meant it. Honest! She had *not* meant it!

Be careful what you wish for …

All of a sudden, she thought of Billy's life insurance policy.

No! She can't think of things like that—not now, anyway. For God's sake, she just found out about his being *dead*!

Amy tried to think of happy memories of Billy. It was a struggle to do so. All that she could remember were the arguments and the belittling she had suffered from Billy.

She began to think about Billy and Ginny's relationship. For the longest time, they had been so close … like a big brother and his little sister … but even closer somehow. He had always been very protective of Ginny.

Could it be? NO! The thought of that was just plain SICK!

From the back of Amy's mind, she began to see images that were taking on new meaning … looks that passed between Ginny and Billy … time that Billy had spent "helping" Ginny out with this or that … the hours that Billy spent on the phone "coaching" Ginny through one of her many, many crises … fights that Amy and Billy would have and Ginny would stick her nose into it, blaming Amy every time … fights that, in retrospect, had been instigated by Ginny.

Oh God … no…no… How could I have been such a fool? It was right there in front of me but I refused to see it.

It was now painfully obvious.

Ginny and Billy had been fooling around. Amy was sure of it. She felt sick. Rage was starting to creep in as she visualized the two of them together. It was disgusting. She hated them both. She was *glad* that Billy was dead. And she was absolutely positive that Ginny had killed him. *That's* who he was meeting up at the falls! They had gone up there before! And she had stupidly *let* them … even *encouraged* Billy to spend "quality time" with her bitch of a little sister! How could Amy have thought it was all so innocent?

They sure must have laughed their heads off at my expense. Did anyone else know? Am I the "last to know"? Why hadn't anyone told me?

She looked around the room and at the disruption that Ginny had caused in so many more ways than what was evident.

Amy had to get out of here. She went upstairs to pack as much of her and the boys' stuff as she could fit into the suitcases they had. She would need to call their landlord. She would *not* be returning to this house!

Ginny was scared. She had never been so scared in her entire life.

Those stupid, ignoramous cops think I killed Billy! I loved him! I would never have done anything to hurt him, let alone kill him, or anyone for that matter. Except for maybe Cassie.

Her rapid-fire thoughts were keeping her from thinking coherently.

Cassie damned-well better have called an attorney. How on earth am I going to pay for a frigging attorney??

She had been in the interrogation room for what seemed like hours.

At least I'm not locked up in a cell! I swear, if I had a gun, I'd shoot myself in the head ... or if I had a rope, I'd hang myself! I don't want to live in this wretched world anymore. I don't care what happens. I just want to go wherever Billy is. Probably hell. We both deserve it.

Is he really DEAD?

The door to the drab, cold room opened. A young man wearing a sports coat and a boldly colored striped tie entered. He looked fresh out of law school, still wet behind the ears.

He pulled a business card from his shirt pocket and handed it to Ginny as he approached the table.

She glanced at it as he told her his name and stuck out his hand.

"Good afternoon, Ms. Miller. I'm Percy Stewart. Your sister, Cassandra, called me on your behalf."

Ginny tentatively took the offered hand.

"It seems that you could use some help," he said.

Ginny broke down into sobs. How could she even have any tears left in her after all the crying she had done over the past few weeks? It seemed impossible, but there were more, lots more.

Young Percy was exceptionally patient as he waited her out.

She finally stopped, drew in a deep breath, and said, "I can't afford an attorney. I don't even have a job. I don't even have a home! I'm homeless!"

He cleared his throat and replied, "Your sister has agreed to take care of your expenses."

"Cassie?!"

"Yes. Cassandra … Cassie."

How could you hate someone *so much* and love them just as strongly at the same time? Ginny's heart swelled. Cassie was looking out for her!

She looked down again at the card in her sweaty hands. She had already somehow pulverized it. It was moist and torn at the edges, but still legible. It read:

The Stewart and Nicholson Firm
Percival Stewart, Attorney at Law

"You have your own firm?"

"It's my father's firm. I've been with them for some time now."

"How long?"

"About a year or so …" He was beginning to sound a little annoyed.

"You just seem so young …"

"Yes." He cut her off. "But I'm qualified to help, if you want me to. Do you want me to?"

"God, YES!"

"Okay then. Let's start at the beginning." He took a seat and pulled a pen out of a leather briefcase with large, branded initials P. S. on the flap. It made Ginny think he had something more to say to the world, like, P. S. I miss you, or, P. S. I don't really know what I'm doing.

"The beginning? The beginning of *what*? Like, when I was arrested?"

"You have not yet been arrested, Ms. Miller. You are merely being detained for questioning. That's why you are in this room—and not in a jail cell."

Ginny's heart quickened. A flicker of hope passed through her. Maybe she wasn't in as much trouble as she thought she was! She suddenly grinned at Percy.

He seemed taken aback by her reaction, but continued.

"Let's start with why you were at the victim's home and why you were tearing the place apart. This fact alone is their probable cause and why you were brought here and detained."

"Really? Yeah, I guess I can kind of see why they might be wondering about that ... I was acting a little crazy."

"Why?"

"Ummm ... well, I had just found out something that made me pretty upset."

"What was that?"

Damn! He wasn't letting her *think*. Ginny had to be very careful here. She did not want to reveal anything about her relationship with Billy. Cassie knew, but considering her own position, she'd probably keep her mouth shut.

"Ms. Miller?"

"Oh! I'm sorry. I just still can't believe that this is all happening."

"Yes, I'm sure. Tell me what it was that made you so upset and why you were at the victim's home."

"Yeah ... Ummm ... I was actually there looking for Billy. I had just found out about a fight that Amy, my sister, and Billy had had. He had twisted her arm ... it really made me mad that he would hurt her ..."

Percy looked dubious.

"My sisters and I are really close ... We are really protective of each other."

"So, your sister and her husband were having some serious problems?"

"I don't know if you'd call them *serious*."

"Serious enough that he would physically assault her?"

"Oh, I know Billy pretty well. I'm sure it wasn't intentional."

"Yet you were angry enough to go and trash their house?"

Her face began to turn red and hot. "Well ... I don't know. I guess I overreacted."

The conversation was not going well.

Percy breathed out a heavy sigh and clicked his pen noisily against the Formica tabletop with a degree of impatience.

"Okay, so that was earlier this afternoon."

Percy looked at his watch. 5:00 p.m. He was getting hungry. This girl was not giving him any answers.

"Why don't you tell me what you did yesterday."

"Yesterday? Saturday? Oh, sure! I was with Cassie all day!"

Ginny's mind was suddenly crystal-clear. She had every minute of every hour of the day accounted for—from an early breakfast through the late-evening hours at the hospital. She had the names of the body shops they had gone to, as well as the written estimates; the names and locations of the apartment complexes they had checked out, and the name of the café where they had eaten lunch. She could even recite what they ate—and surely Cassie still had the receipt!

"So, these people at all these places would be able to vouch for you and your sister for your whereabouts all day?"

"Absolutely! Even the apartment managers made a copy of my driver's license before letting us see any of the apartments."

Ginny was excited to have such a detailed accounting of her day.

The day in question.

Percy still looked dubious.

He was quiet as he contemplated her story; she watched him carefully as he thought.

She was barely able to contain herself.

"So you see? I COULDN'T have killed Billy! I was way too busy!"

He looked at Ginny like she was some kind of a fruitcake, but said,

"Well, it looks as though they have no reason to detain you after all, as long as you have an explanation of your whereabouts and such an iron-clad alibi ... Wait here, and I'll see about getting you released."

He got up and left the room, taking his noisy pen with him.

Ginny felt as free as a bird as she exited the police station. Thank the Lord above that she had such an iron-clad alibi, and her recounting of her day had been astonishing. She had even impressed herself.

Despite her feelings of elation, her heart still sat like a heavy stone somewhere in her bowels. There was just no way that Billy could be *dead*.

How could this be true?

As she walked down the steps and reached the sidewalk, she realized her car was still parked at Amy and Billy's house.

God damn it.

She reached into her pocket for her cell phone, but came up empty.

Did I leave it in the car? I always keep it in that pocket.

She did not want to go back into the station to use a phone, so she began to walk down the street in the direction of her mother's house. It would probably take twenty minutes to get there by foot, but she needed time to think anyway. As she passed other occasional pedestrians, they appeared somewhat alarmed as they looked at her in passing. She realized just how bad she must look, and kept her head down as she progressed towards Mom's. She breathed a sigh of relief as she entered the house, ignoring Cassie, who sat at the kitchen table in what looked to be a state of shock. Ginny's arrival did not seem to register.

Ginny made her way to the upstairs bathroom, passing by Amy's bedroom, in which Will and Bobby made mournful cries. She ignored them too. She desperately needed a long, hot bath. That was all she was capable of at this point.

The next few days were spent in a fog for the three sisters. Nobody knew what to say to each other. Ginny disappeared to her apartment to start packing her possessions in order to move back to Mom's house. Amy was on autopilot, preparing meals and trying to maintain some semblance of normalcy for the kid's sake; though absolutely nothing was normal in their lives, and they all knew it. She had been given as much time off work as she needed, but almost wished she could be there instead of here. She had not heard word one from Geoffrey ... no concern, no sympathy, no nothing.

She made funeral arrangements with a business-like attitude and countenance. She was numb.

Cassie just tried to stay out of Amy's way. She was itching to tell Amy everything she knew, thinking that it might help Amy; as well as to hopefully relieve her own conscience. But Amy was so blank, so vacant. It seemed she was nothing but a shell.

The police had come by several times with questions, and then more questions. The three sisters were steadfast in their stories, giving nothing away despite their suspicions of each other. They verbally supported each other in a way that they never had before. The police had no reason to think that any one of the three had done Billy in, let alone had a motive. It was a mystery.

Finally, Percy Stewart notified Ginny that the police believed Billy had been involved in a drug deal gone bad. There was a large wad of money found in his pocket, as well as pot, liquor, and other miscellaneous drugs stuffed in his backpack found at the top of the landing. The early and unprecedented thaw due to warm weather made it virtually impossible to collect any hard evidence. Unless some new evidence surfaced, the police would be following the drug deal scenario, but it wasn't looking hopeful that they would solve it. Ginny called Amy and Cassie to report what her attorney had revealed.

None of them felt relief, just confusion.

Answers would have at least provided some comfort. Somehow, they all knew that the police were wrong, but hell would freeze over before they let that be known.

The funeral was almost embarrassing. Amy, Cassie, and Ginny sat together in the first row, along with Will and Bobby. There were a few coworkers and old school acquaintances, but it was obvious that Billy had no friends. He had also had no family other than these three badly treated women and two sons. The only tears shed were by the two young boys that Billy had left behind, and one Amazon-like, red-headed woman who must have worked with Billy, but Amy did not even know. The woman disappeared at the end of the service without talking to anyone; not that Amy wanted to talk with anyone anyway.

The whole thing was surreal.

Amy made daily visits to the hospital to check on Mom. She knew that both Cassie and Ginny were also making visits, but for some reason, they did not go together.

Despite working with all the various therapists: physical, speech, and occupational, Mom was making no progress; although she wasn't deteriorating either.

Until.

It was a few days after the funeral. Ginny had moved into Mom's house with Amy, Cassie, and the boys. They were sitting around the kitchen table, picking at the chicken-pot-pie and the broccoli casserole provided by Beverly, who had taken pity on the dysfunctional and morbid family, and was coming over daily to do what she could. She was there in the kitchen with them, tidying things up, not knowing what else to do for them.

The phone suddenly rang out shrilly in the silence punctuated by forks clinking on plates.

Cassie went to answer it.

"Hello?"

Her face lit up.

"Seriously?" she said to the caller.

Amy and Ginny stopped eating, forks halfway to their mouths.

"We'll be right there," said Cassie, as she hung up the receiver. "Mom's talking! She's coming back around!"

"What?"

"You're kidding!"

"Let's go!"

They scurried to get it together and jumped into Amy's car, leaving the boys under Beverly's supervision.

As Amy pulled out of the driveway, she muttered, "It's about time something good happened in this family."

Neither Cassie nor Ginny responded.

"And don't *either* of you say anything that could upset Mom! Don't tell her anything about what's happened. Who knows what it could do to her? She loved Billy."

"Don't worry, Amy, we won't. Don't you think that we want what's best for Mom too?" Ginny's retort was smart-alecky, but held a note of optimism at the same time.

Cassie chimed in, "I don't think any of us want to upset Mom. Hurry, Amy, drive faster."

Amy sped up, but would only go three or four miles over the limit.

"Getting a speeding ticket certainly won't make us get there any faster," she primly stated.

Cassie and Ginny rolled their eyes at each other, but grinned.

The feeling in the car was anticipatory as they made their way toward Mercy.

~

They could see the difference in their mother as soon as they entered her room. She had been transferred down to the rehab unit several days ago and the room itself was friendlier; almost like a hotel room rather than a hospital room. Also, Mom was wearing her own sleeping gown and robe instead of hospital garb—but that wasn't it. It was in her eyes. There was an awareness that had been missing for the past couple of weeks. Recognition was a beautiful sight to behold, and all three girls cried as they clamored around their mother, hugging her as though they hadn't seen her in years.

In their excitement, the questions tumbled out of their mouths.

"How do you feel?"

"Do you know what happened?"

"Do you know where you are?"

"Mom, do you know who we are?"

Until Amy shushed them.

"Don't overwhelm her. One at a time. Mom? Do you know who I am?"

Janice struggled, but managed a weak half-smile and said, "Amy," as she reached out her right hand to touch her eldest daughter's cheek. Amy hugged her again.

"And me, Mom … what about me?"

Janice's eyes shifted, and then settled on Ginny. The same struggle to smile and speak.

"Ginny," as her hand moved to Ginny's face.

"What about *me*, Mom?" Cassie pushed her way in front of Ginny.

The process repeated and Janice managed Cassie's name as well.

It was a miracle. They all laughed.

"This is amazing! How come, all of a sudden, she can do this?" Amy asked Ginny.

"I don't know … it just works this way sometimes. Mom's lucky. Therapy doesn't always bring about changes like this."

"Where … Will … Boh … Boh …"

"Will and Bobby are at home, Mom. Beverly is watching them," interrupted Amy.

"Amy, you really should give Mom time to finish her thoughts and her words," advised Ginny.

"Yeah … okay." Amy continued smiling at her mother despite being told what to do by Ginny.

"Can she come home? Mom, do you want to come home?" asked Cassie.

Again, Ginny had her two cents.

"Don't rush things, Cassie … She's not ready."

But Mom was answering, saying, "Yes … Home …"

The girls were at a loss as to how to respond. Of course Mom would want to come home. But could she? Was she ready? How on earth could they tell her, *not yet*? Would she understand? Would she get upset?

As they grappled with what to say, Mom spoke again.

"Billy … okay?"

The girls glanced nervously at each other. Why would Mom be asking if Billy was okay? Had someone told her about what had happened?

Amy spat out at her sisters in a whisper, "Did either of you tell her anything?"

"God, no!"

"Of course not!"

Mom wasn't deaf. She watched and listened to the interchange with an increased look of alarm on her face.

She spoke again.

"Billy … fell … hurt."

The three sisters suddenly wore identical expressions of surprise and shock; brows raised, eyes wide, mouths open …

Amy responded first.

"Mom, how do you know that Billy fell?"

"I … I … saw … him." She appeared agitated as she fought to express herself.

"Billy … ff … ff … *fell.* Rocks."

"How could she know this?" Amy hissed at her sisters. They were dumbfounded.

"Billy… hurt … my … my … *poor girls.* I … st … stop Billy … *monster.*"

Janice was becoming very agitated.

"Mom, calm down. It's okay, please …"

Amy was stuck between wanting to comfort her mother and finding out exactly what Janice knew.

Amy, Cassie, and Ginny looked from one to the other and back at Mom.

This was bizarre.

Could Mom have been there at the falls?

Ginny ventured, "Do you guys remember how we found her wet, filthy clothes under the bed the day she had the stroke? The same day Billy died? And remember the way Cassie's car was parked all weird in the driveway with the door wide open?"

Their minds were firing on all cylinders, disbelief and comprehension dawning on all three of them at the same time.

Could *Mom* have been the one to have met Billy at the falls?

But why on earth?

How on earth?

What exactly did she know about this?

Amy took control.

"Mom … Mom, were you there, at the waterfalls when Billy … ummmm … *fell?*"

"Yu … Yu … *YES,*" Janice sputtered and then broke into tears.

"Amy, this can't be good for her. Maybe we should let it go for now …" ventured Cassie.

"But we need to find out *what happened,*" added Ginny.

"Let's just give her a minute to calm down," said Amy. "Obviously, I want to know whatever she knows …"

"We *all* do," said Cassie.

They looked at each other with a newfound sense of trust. Their previous suspicions concerning the details of Billy's death were being thwarted by Mom's semi-confession … or explanation … whatever it was.

Mom went from hitting at the blanket with her right hand, to picking at it. Her tears subsided and she looked questioningly at her three daughters.

Amy began again, treading very cautiously.

"Mom? Are you all right?"

Janice managed a half-smile. The left sided droop a reminder of the stroke she had suffered.

"Mom, *why* were you there at the falls with Billy?"

"To help … my … p … p … poor girls!" and she started to tear up again, drool running down her chin.

"What does she mean, 'to help my poor girls'?" asked Cassie.

"Well how should *I* know?" shot back Amy.

They looked helplessly at their mother, waiting for her to say something more. Ginny had begun to fidget noticeably.

"Is … Billy … all … all … right?"

"Tell her the truth Amy," demanded Ginny.

"Jesus, Ginny. Give her a break, would ya?" interrupted Cassie.

"Ssshhh," hissed Amy at her sisters.

"Mom? Billy got hurt … you know, when he fell. Did you see him fall? Did anyone push him?"

Janice shook her head. "Acc … acci … dent. Slip … and … fall. Ju … just me … mon-mon-monster … Billy … *monster*." Her face was flushed to a deep crimson.

"Stop," said Ginny flatly. "I think I know what happened."

"What do you mean, you know what happened? How could *you* know what happened?"

"Amy … umm … we need to talk, but not here. Not now. Just stop questioning Mom about this, *please*."

"What the hell, Ginny?"

"Please. I think I can make some sense of all this … just give me a chance to explain."

She suddenly changed her tone and demeanor. "Mom? Can I get you anything?"

Another lopsided smile, making the girls wince.

The silence in the room was deafening, broken by Janice repeating her question, "Billy … all right?"

"For Christ's sake. NO, Mom! He's not all right already! He's DEAD! He died at the falls!" Ginny's sudden outburst startled them all, and then she fled from the room.

Amy immediately put her arms around her mother as Janice's face had gone white with Ginny's words.

Amy stroked the old woman's head. "Ssshhhh .... ssshhh. It's all right." She looked over the fuzzy gray hair at Cassie, who stood with eyes and mouth agape.

At that moment, a nurse rushed in, responding to the ruckus.

"What's going on in here?" she demanded. "Your mother is in no condition to handle being upset."

"I know. I know. We're so sorry ... Ginny just got mad at me. Please, it's okay ..." Amy attempted to explain as she continued to stroke her mother's head.

"Maybe you should go now and let her get a good night's sleep."

"Yes. Of course ..."

Amy held Janice out at arm's length to look at her. Not only was her face still as white as a sheet, but her eyes had taken on a glassy appearance, all remnants of the previous recognition totally gone.

"WHAT'S WRONG WITH HER!?" screeched Cassie.

The nurse quickly made her way to the side of the bed.

"Janice? Janice? Can you hear me?" The nurse reached for Janice's wrist to check her pulse. A troubled expression washed over her.

"WHAT'S WRONG WITH HER!?" repeated Cassie.

"I'm not sure, but I think she's had another stroke."

Ginny was breathing hard when she entered the empty family waiting area. She had been holding *so much* in for *so long*. Her suspicions, her doubts, her guilt. It was literally driving her crazy.

And now this?

Mom had BEEN THERE!

Just as she had suspected. But, Mom hadn't pushed Billy at all—he *fell*!

The fact that she had even considered that her mother was capable of such a horrible thing made Ginny feel … feel … GOD! Ginny didn't know *what* to feel anymore.

She had never even entertained the thought of telling the police about the voice mail she found and listened to on her cell phone. In fact, she had deleted it, permanently. Billy's last call incriminated *Ginny* more than anyone, and they already had reason to suspect her!

Why did things like this always have to happen to *her*?

She wished she had her own car here. All she wanted to do was to get out of this bad luck hospital. She could swear there were evil forces at work against her in this God-forsaken place.

She was still breathing hard.

At least now Ginny could tell Amy and Cassie about the phone call. It all made sense now … Mom had gone to the falls to protect Amy… from *Ginny*.

Oh God, Amy is going to hate me!

Three Months Later

"Who'da thunk it?" murmured Cassie out of the blue.

Cassie, Amy, and Ginny were sitting around the kitchen table playing a game of SORRY.

"Who'da thunk what?" asked Ginny distractedly.

"That we would all end up living in our childhood home … *together*!"

Amy was focused on the task at hand. She had more of her pieces closer to the home stretch than either of her sisters, and it looked as if she was going to win this game.

She looked up and said matter-of-factly,

"It was meant to be."

Nobody responded. Amy believed in things like that … signs, fate, destiny.

Mom had not made it through the night after her second stroke. The doctor had explained that sometimes a patient would have a freak, but brief improvement, followed by a sudden decline. You just never knew.

Ginny had taken Mom's death exceptionally hard. She had been aware of the message from Billy to meet her up at the falls, and knew it had been listened to prior to her hearing it. Since she had left her phone at Mom's house that awful day, she had a strong suspicion that Mom had heard the message, but had truly thought it impossible that her mother would actually have made the trek to the falls.

Ginny's guilt was already too much to bear. Not only did she feel responsible for Mom going to the falls in the first place, but she also felt responsible for Mom's second stroke after Ginny had so callously told her about Billy's death.

She was bound and determined to turn over a new leaf and become a kinder, more thoughtful human being. So far, it was working. Her extreme contrition had made it possible for even Amy to find some forgiveness in her heart.

It was odd, but over the past weeks, Ginny had become increasingly dependent on Amy … almost childlike. It was as if she were projecting her emotions and replacing the loss of her mother with Amy. The thing was, Amy not only didn't mind, but seemed to thrive on this change in their relationship. Amy was doing a great job filling Mom's shoes in Mom's house. It was uncanny how much like her mother Amy actually was.

The whole thing about Billy and Ginny, and Billy and Cassie, and even Billy and Amy, was all out in the open. There were no more secrets. The day of the big revelation just happened to coincide with Amy's learning that the funds from Billy's life insurance would be released to her. She had been livid when she discovered he had cancelled his policy, but then elated to find out that his death had occurred during the grace period. Her sudden wealth must have had an influence on her understanding and forgiving attitude toward her two sisters.

Mom had left the house to her three daughters, and they had subsequently agreed to live together in the big, rambling home that they knew so well. Each sibling took back her old bedroom, and the boys shared Mom's. At first, Amy had worried that her sons might feel spooked, so she had transformed the bedroom with fresh paint, new curtains, and new furniture—a sports theme. Their twin beds had headboards that looked like basketball goals, baskets and all! They loved it. Their moments of mourning for their departed father were becoming farther and fewer between. Life moved on.

As the grief continued to lift over the weeks following Mom's death, a sort of peacefulness took its place. It was as though the animosity that had existed between the three girls got buried right along with Billy.

"I've been thinking ..." said Amy, as she moved her third piece into the HOME spot, after drawing a "two" card.

Cassie and Ginny looked up at her.

"Well, Ginny, you still don't have a job, and you can't work as a nurse anymore anyway ... and Cassie, you *hate* your job ..."

"Yeah, so?"

"What are you thinking, Amy?"

"What if we used some of the life insurance money I got and opened up a cute little gift shop? We could specialize in handmade crafts. I could teach you how to make so many nice things—it would be fun! We could all run it together ... I think we'd really love it!"

This was the first time since the family tragedies that anyone had sounded either animated or excited about anything, and it was contagious.

"I think that's a GREAT idea, Amy!" chirped Cassie.

"You know ... I think it could work!" responded Ginny.

"It's settled then!"

The euphoric silence was interrupted by Amy.

"I guess Billy really *was* worth more dead," she said quietly as she studied the gameboard, and then moved her final piece into the Home spot.

"I won!"

And then she looked back up at her sisters with a bit of a smile and said, "*Tsk ...tsk.*"

About the Author

ANNE KATHERYN HAWLEY grew up along the rocky coast of New England. She comes from a family of ten, where she often collects the "grains" that sprout within her imagination and grow into stories.

She attended Belmont College in Nashville, Tennessee. In addition to writing novels, she is a portrait artist, a fiddle player, and works part-time as a registered nurse.

She is married and has two children. She currently lives among the tall pines and crystal-clear lakes of Northern Michigan.